Table of Contents

THE MONSTER GASPED, OMG!

Welcome Letter from
Brentano Math & Science Academy

Dear Monster Reader:

OMG, what an adventure! Thanks to 826CHI and their superb volunteers, Brentano's fourth and fifth grade students developed and published original stories about monsters, beasts, and mythical creatures. Just like someone reading a good intro, our students were hooked from the start. Anxiety turned to excitement right from their first discussion of favorite superpowers: "Telekinesis! Super speed! Teleportation!" they exulted. Every Tuesday after that, students rushed to class asking, "826CHI is coming today, *right?!*"

The 826CHI staff and volunteers partnered with the Brentano team to help students with mini-lessons on story arcs, figurative language, dialogue, word choice, and many other narrative writing essentials. A riveting theme, plus enthusiasm, teamwork, and a unique approach to teaching writing combined to make this an experience our students will remember all their lives.

Beware—our students' stories will have you laughing and gasping. Thank you, and enjoy.

Sincerely,

Seth Lavin, *Principal*
Mark Harlan, *Teacher*

Letter from the Student Editorial Board

Good Day, Fellow Monster:

If you turn the page, it will be the most legendary thing that will ever happen to you, because you're about to unleash the monsters in this book.

There are many twists and turns: a monster with the power of destruction and eyes that cry spicy tears; a girl put in jail for asking a question; a king who gets captured because he's old; a story about a half-sheep, half-guy, and National Donut Day—because who would not want donuts falling from the sky? If you don't like one of the small stories you're reading, you can just turn to another story instead of using your time looking for another book, because all the stories are unique and you never know what's going to happen.

A lot of imagination and excitement was put into this book, and that's what you need for a good story. The easiest thing is when you have an idea. The hardest is when you don't. You need imagination, creativity, and experience—if you don't have an imagination, *imaginate* that you have an imagination. You have to do a lot of thinking and sometimes you think it's not good enough, and it's difficult coming up with another idea without copying or reenacting people's books or movies. So don't put this book down so easily, because you don't know how hard it was.

This is an extraordinary book because it's like the monsters are right there in front of you acting it out. You can learn a lot from this radical book. It teaches us how people react to abnormal events and that you shouldn't judge someone by their look, but by their personality. You'll want to read these wondrous stories so you can change perspectives. In many stories and movies, they make the monster a villain and we took the chance to make the monster the hero of the story. Just like there are some people who are bad guys and some who aren't—in some of our stories, monsters are the good guys and in some they're the bad guys. These stories teach us that we're like monsters and we're all different. Monsters and humans both hate and love and are sad and scared and disgusted. Some of us play video games and some like to read; some are funny, some are smart; some of us are strong—but we hold the same feelings. These stories will remind you of yourself.

Anyway, it was exciting and we had fun writing it—and sometime, you should try to write a story.

Brace yourself. You're about to unleash extraordinary magic. We've warned you.

The Student Editorial Board:
Lilliana M. Harris
Joshua Parsio
Chris Guedes
Kayla Santiago
Alondra Ruvalcaba
Marvin Lazo
Silva Flores
Maurice Edwards
Vanessa Benavides
Emily Drzewiecki

Imagination and the Necessity of the Unknown

by JOE MENO

Everything we ever end up knowing ends up only being a guess. The birth of the universe, the basic building blocks of nature, the scope of all fauna and flora on Earth, who we are as people, and why do we exist—all these answers on which we have built an entire world are really only what we imagine to be true. We have some very reasonable ideas about the nature of ourselves and the nature of the universe but, in the end, the things we feel, the things we believe, have little to do with any known facts.

•

As a first grade student, I was terrible. I drew in a spiral notebook all day, scrawling pictures of as-yet-engineered tanks fighting wholly imagined dinosaurs. Sometimes a wizard or two would appear and make things difficult for the army who had enough problems with the dinosaurs. When it was time for a spelling test or a math test, I'd draw the same dinosaurs eating the questions. Superheroes surrounded by lightning bolts or skeleton armies were sometimes my only answers. I know now these were my earliest attempts at telling stories. I did not have the language yet to write out what was in my head and I did not do well in school until I learned that stories—whether stories in science or math or history—are what really matter. Because stories change the very nature of things.

•

The other day, driving home, I heard a story on the radio that there might be a hidden planet in our solar system. I almost had to pull over. I am a 41-one year old person but I got so excited I almost crashed. Why? Because I had grown up in the 1970s and 1980s and the entire universe was defined as a very specific series of nine planets orbiting a very bright orange sun. We each made a model in fifth grade out of Styrofoam and hung them up in our classrooms, 26 suns, 26 earths, 26 solar systems all dangling above our heads. In this way, or by accident, this depiction of the world beyond our planet, an expansive and unknowable series of unnamed planets, was actually closer to the truth. There is much more that we don't know than we do, worlds upon worlds hidden from our own.

•

I had a bad case of strep throat when I was eight. I was stuck in bed for a few days and my dad—a man of few words—brought me home three comic books. In these imaginative, impossible tales of super-humans, reanimated dinosaurs, and aliens, I learned all I needed to know about how the world worked, that what you can imagine can actually turn out to be true. I began to understand that make-believe stories—whether science fiction, horror, or fantasy—are where some of our best ideas come from. Whether we're discussing the birth of aviation, medicine, space-travel, technology, everything from rocket ships to iPhones to genetic coding, what we're talking about is fiction writers coming up with bold ideas that help shape and redefine our lives. It's the fiction writer's job to imagine what can be instead of what is and help us reimagine our place in the universe.

•

This is exactly why the stories contained within *The Monster Gasped, OMG!* are the best, the absolutely best kind of stories. They allow us to see the world as a place of infinite possibilities. There are a number of impossible journeys like "Smelly Socks, Old Toys, and Another Dimension: Things I Found Under My Bed," by Kayla Santiago, in which the narrator travels to another planet through a door in the floor. There are dangerous scientific experiments like "Tsunami the Big Blue Fish," by Emily Drzewiecki in which a fish goes through several mysterious transformations. There's even the uncanny appearances of magical creatures like in "Who's There?" by Ruby Echeandia, in which a red-eyed demon with fangs hides in a bush and tries to steal unsuspecting victims. Everything we have ever wanted to know about the necessity of exploring the unknown is described here within these pages.

•

In some important ways, I have never given up believing in the impossible. It's the reason I still have any sense of hope. When I hear about a hidden planet, I begin to think: What might it be called? What does it look like? How might this change everything?

•

Read these stories and be prepared to believe.

The Rise of Haley

by CHRIS GUEDES

ne day, a very long time ago, a great mistake was made: Haley. From the second she was born, Haley ran away from the doctor, her mom, and her dad. One day, Haley was in a kid's room crawling up her wall on four legs, her wrinkly face and dry hair slumped over, when the kid saw her.

"AAAAAHHHH!"

"Don't say anything, kid, or else I'll get you."

"OK, OK pl-pl-pl-please don't h-h-hur-hur-hurt me."

When Haley started to grow, she studied The Ghost of Madden a lot. The Ghost of Madden was born from nothing and lived underground in the dirt. Every day people would walk by arguing and fighting, which brought up this evil spirit. He had huge feet, old ripped up clothes, and carried around a fiery dagger. Haley grew more interested; she studied and watched conspiracies of The Ghost of Madden. She decided she wanted to work for him. Haley asked her friend to help her.

"Hey, I want to work for The Ghost of Madden."

"OK, you need help filling out the paperwork?"

"Yes."

"OK, I'll help you."

"Thank you."

Haley made her way to the deep, dark, fiery cave of lava to meet The Ghost of Madden and be his sidekick. Haley was waiting in line. She saw The Ghost of Madden and yelled, "Please hire me!"

"No, don't hire her, hire me!" a huge ghost goat interrupted.

"He's right. Get out, now!" The Ghost of Madden demanded.

"But, but, but . . . fine," Haley hissed.

Haley tried again.

"Please hire me," said Haley.

"No, hire me. I'm way stronger," said Huge Snake Boy. He smelled like a street alley that had rotten old garbage cans and a sewer.

"Yeah, I pick him. Get out," The Ghost of Madden said.

The third time she went back to The Ghost of Madden, he said no again, but Haley made him a deal: "If I can collect four spirits in five days, you have to let me be your assistant."

"Deal," The Ghost of Madden said.

Haley went house to house, grabbing spirits. Finally, she was done and was working for The Ghost of Madden.

She fell in love with him. She asked The Ghost of Madden to marry her. He said no. She left angrily. She came back later that day. She knew that The Ghost of Madden had a secret— he hated the numbers 19, 30, 32, and 8.

When he first arose from underground, those were the very first words he heard. Some- one was taking down a phone number after arguing over the phone. Haley came back to his cave and yelled, "19, 30, 32, 8!" The Ghost of Madden collapsed. The Ghost of Madden, lying hurt, said, "Good luck. You'll need it." Then it disintegrated and faded away into sparks.

Haley was the new overpowering ruler of the deep, dark, fiery cave of lava. She takes spirits whenever she can. The town needs to prepare for Haley.

Apocalipsis

by MELODY DORANTES

nce, there was an old lady who had a young child whose name was Stella. Stella was always getting into trouble at school.

"A time out?" cried Stella, shocked. "I'm too old for that!"

Stella had broken a neighbor's window with a rock because she was so mad.

One day, Stella noticed that there was a sound coming from her closet. Out of her closet came a hideous and terrifying monster named Apocalipsis! The monster was green with pink spikes on its back, and it was big enough to fit in Stella's closet. The monster screamed and tried to pounce on Stella.

From that day forward, Stella was always scared to sleep in her room. Apocalipsis, on the other hand, thought that she was a hideous human and was afraid she would make that hideous screech that humans make when they are scared.

One day, the monster attempted to talk to the child and became best friends with her.

"Hello," whimpered Apocalipsis.

"Hello?" questioned Stella. The monster and Stella talked about their pasts and what kinds of candies they liked.

Then, Stella had to move to a new house.

"I have to move!" said Stella in anger. So the monster was left with no friends.

Apocalipsis tried to make friends with the next child, named Zoe.

"Hello," the monster urged.

"I know that you are in my closet," said Zoe.

Zoe became an angry troll since the lights in the house were as bright as the sun, and she sent the monster to a distant planet called Zerd.

It took 10 seconds to get to planet Zerd.

"NOOOO!" screamed the monster.

MMM,
CANDY!
I'M GOING
TO EAT
IT!

Soon, Apocalipsis discovered that the planet had glowing blue water with very big craters, candy trees, and marshmallow bushes. But the strange thing was that there was a big house made with candy, gumdrops, and Lay's barbecue chips for a roof! The lights were on but nobody was home.

It seemed like a monster had been there, but long ago. A monster made of candy. Apocalipsis found marshmallow coals. There was a lot of food and three different bags of candy, like Sour Patch Kids, gumdrops, gummy bears, Skittles, Hershey's, jawbreakers, gum, Swedish Fish, and cotton candy.

"Mmm, candy! I'm going to eat it!" said Apocalipsis.

There was a bed upstairs and the monster got tired, so he laid down. "I am so tired," yawned Apocalipsis.

The monster had a dream that he was playing with Stella.

"Stella!" the monster said as he woke up. He wanted to find his way back to Earth. "It is so isolated here on Zerd. I do not like it," groaned the monster. "I have to get back to Stella."

The monster did not think he could find a way to get back to Earth for a long time. But then, Apocalipsis made a machine of candy and pressed a marshmallow button to let out energy.

"I hope this works . . . It worked! I am back on Earth!"

Malana's Dream Came True

by GIMARY VILLATORO

nce upon a time there was a girl named Malana who was born in a cemetery. Malana turned 15 just 10 minutes after being born! Everybody in her family did that. They were not quite sure why. Malana was fashionable. She wore a shirt that said "Flesh Plz." She had a sparkling blue skirt and also had black hair that was in two braids.

Malana tried to find somewhere to live. She saw an open door in a dirty alley full of rats and junk and shouted, "I wish I was invisible," and *BAM!* She turned invisible.

There, Malana found a pink room inside the house and went inside the closet. She decided that was where she was going to live. She saw everybody in the house and they saw her, and immediately they left because they were terrified. She felt hungry, so she ate a whole chicken, to which Malana admitted, "Yum, that was delicious!"

Then she went to the living room. That's when everything changed. She saw a movie that was about this doll named Austin! Austin had blonde hair, a white shirt, and black jeans. He was also a monster.

"OMG he is soooo cute!" She fell in love with him. She decorated her house with Austin dolls. Malana felt pretty lonely, so she stole a dog and kept it. She named it Cookie.

"Cookie is the perfect name for you," she blurted out.

One day, Cookie got injured because Malana accidentally threw a vase, and it fell on top of Cookie's leg. Malana giggled, "Oops." But then Malana took her to the vet, and Cookie was all better.

One day, Malana got tickets to go and meet Austin. Someone was selling them on the streets for $40, so she bought one.

"Ahhh, I can't wait!" she screamed.

She was excited until she noticed that Austin's sister, Carla, the baddest villain, was also planning to go meet Austin! Carla had red skin and black clothes. She had once tried to en-slave everyone around her, but she messed up on her plan.

"Oh, no." She didn't want to go anymore. But then Malana declared, "This is my biggest dream. I have to do it!"

So she did. She had to walk from Chicago to Florida to meet Austin, because nobody let her go on a bus, train, or taxi since she was a monster. Ten hours passed and Malana was so tired, she fell asleep in the middle of the forest. Then she woke up and 15 more hours had passed and she was very hungry, so she stopped off at a restaurant. She kept on walking. Seventeen more hours passed. She had to walk through the forest, and she had to meet Austin in one hour.

"Cookie, I think I am going to faint!" Malana exclaimed.

Malana was walking with her dog until *BOOM!* A cage fell on top of her.

"I knew it."

She saw Carla, Austin's sister, come out of nowhere. Malana was frightened. She knew something like this was going to happen. Then, Austin came for Malana.

Malana told her dog, "Cookie, catch me if I faint."

Austin told his sister, "How could you?"

Carla responded, "I don't care! It's my job, I'm the baddest villain in the WORLD!"

Malana had pepper spray, so she sprayed it in Carla's eyes. Austin and Malana left togeth-er. They were together the whole day.

Malana stated, "This was the best day of my life."

Austin said, "It was the best day of my life, too."

Then, they kissed! Malana almost fainted.

"I . . . I can't believe I just did that," gasped Malana.

At that moment, Austin got down on one knee.

ILLUSTRATOR: COLE BLOTKY / STUDENT: CHRIS GUEDES, PAGE 19

The Lion on Fire

by MAURICE EDWARDS

ILLUSTRATOR: KEARA MCGRAW / STUDENT: SKY JIMENEZ, PAGE 29

ong ago there was a baby lion named Simpix, but in lion years he was 10 years old. His family was carried away by hunters and he was left all alone by himself. He looked like a lion mixed with a bird on fire. His mane was bright red like a tomato and his wings were big and bright.

Five years later, Simpix was with his friends going to a fireproof movie theater. It was for animals and meta-humans like him who could not control their fire yet. They all watched the movie *Fireman*. The movie was about a guy who caught fire, got powers from the fire, and had to save the world from Dr. Meow and Dr. Rilla. They were the bad guys.

Simpix and his friends watched the movie in peace for two hours and 30 minutes. After the movie, they went off to go hunt for their food (but they ate it cooked, not raw). After that, Simpix went home to go to sleep but three sheriffs tried to hunt him because Simpix had almost burned down their town.

"Where is he?" asked the first sheriff.

"Stop talking!" commanded the other sheriff.

"I think we should split up," suggested the third sheriff.

The three sheriffs tried to hunt him, but then a boy wandered toward a volcano. This was Simpix's volcano.

"Wow, look at this volcano!" remarked the boy. Then, he fell! "Aaaaaaaaaa ahhhhhhhhh! I'm falling! Help!" yelled the boy.

The kid was saved by Simpix because he flew in to catch the boy. Simpix can turn off his fire so he feels chilly. It can stay off for six minutes only. He flew back to the town with the boy.

"You saved him?" asked the sheriff.

"Yes, I did," replied Simpix.

The whole town shouted, "Yeah, he's a good guy!"

"Here's a fireproof medal for rescuing the little boy and being an idol," beamed the mayor.

"Thanks," said Simpix. They were on the stage in downtown New York, with a big Simpix picture in the background.

Snake the Rat's Life at School

by SKY JIMENEZ

 husband and wife were expecting a baby, but the husband was a rat and the wife was a snake. Their baby was going to be mixed up into a snake blended with a rat. When the wife and husband had their baby, they named it Snake the Rat.

The mom sang, "I can't wait for the baby to love me and care for me." Snake the Rat was green and had red eyes, long hair, and a really long tail and tongue.

When Snake the Rat was three years old, his parents died and he had no one to stay with him. He almost died because he did not have anything to eat or drink, and he started to cry because his parents had died. He had to get himself into school and find a house, because his house was starting to deteriorate. But his new house was so cold he almost froze to death!

At his new school, he got bullied because he was different from all the other monsters. But he had to go to monster school, or else the humans would make fun of him even more. No one knew that he was getting bullied, because he had no one to turn to. He would say that his parents were home, but they were not. He just had to walk to his freezing home and try his best to do his homework without any help. When Snake was coming home, people would yell, "You are so stupid. Just die already, you crater-faced monster." When people called him that, he felt so dumb.

Most of the time, he would get his homework wrong since he had no one to help him. His teachers did not like him, so he couldn't ask for help. He had no friends, not even one. He would often just cry because no one liked or talked to him. He sometimes went to Warbucks and drank a Frappuccino to calm down.

Josh, a well-known bully, was purple and loved to eat computers. He lurked around and wanted to fight Snake the Rat. When Snake went to the playground, Josh yelled, "Why are you even walking around? Just go home. No one likes you, so just leave."

When Snake heard that, he was about to fight Josh but stated, "No, I am not going to leave. You are not the boss of me."

When Josh heard that, he punched Snake, and Snake fell to the ground. Then he kicked Josh in the face.

After recess, the teachers articulated, "You guys are in so, so, so much trouble! Especially you, Josh, because you started the fight. But since Snake has no parents, he will not get in so much trouble."

When Josh got in more trouble than Snake, he got so mad he tried to beat Snake up again.

When Snake came to school the next day, he was really sad because he'd gotten into a fight. At lunch, Snake tried to apologize, but Josh scolded, "I forgive you, but I will not talk to you, because I am still mad at you."

They were now enemies. But Josh had wanted to be Snake's friend all along.

One day, Snake was walking and Josh went up to him and uttered, "I am sorry for bullying you and fighting with you. I lost all my friends because they thought that I was too mean. I was thinking that we need each other."

Snake sighed, "I forgive you so much! Let's go get something to eat, because I am so hungry."

"OK!"

One stormy morning, Josh told his parents he wanted a brother, because he did not have one. So they asked him, "Who did you have in mind?"

Josh replied, "I was thinking Snake, because he has no parents." His parents told him they'd see what they could do.

Josh saw Snake walking to Warbucks and he gasped, "My mom told me that she might be able to adopt you, and you might become my brother!"

Snake was hoping that he would get adopted by Josh's parents. The next day, Josh's mom and dad came to Snake's house to pick him up to adopt him.

Their parents were thinking of having a party to introduce Snake to the rest of the family. Later on, all the family came, and they had the biggest party in the world.

When the party was over, Snake was thinking about what his parents would say if they were alive.

Scared to Change

by EMILY ARROYO

here was a wolf named Rex who was brown, had blue eyes, and was 6 feet tall. He had sharp white teeth and claws. Rex had pointy ears and big, red eyes. He lived in a dark forest where it was snowy, and the only sounds that could be heard were his loud growls and howls. Sometimes you could hear him running through the trees. Everyone was scared to enter the forest. He was mean to the other wolves and bit people so they would not enter the forest.

One day, Rex found a cave and jumped in to see what he could find. Rocks fell from above and he couldn't get out. Rex was trapped!

Now he was the one who was scared. Rex kept howling and howling, louder and louder. A couple of wolves heard him. They looked down into the cave and found him. The wolves didn't really want to help Rex because he had been so mean to them in the past.

"Please help me! I'm sorry that I was so mean to you guys!" Rex cried.

"We will help you if you promise to never be mean to us again," replied the wolves.

The wolves decided to trust Rex and helped him out of the cave. Rex was so happy he hugged them all! He was cheerful and went back home. Rex changed from being mean to being helpful and nice to others, forever and always.

The Trapped Parents

by MIA TOLAYO

oJo was a Tiger Spider. She had eight legs and tiger stripes on her back. Her stripes were black but her fur was brown, and she had white eyes. She, like all other Tiger Spiders, was as big as a newborn baby. JoJo was always nice and happy, and was always looking out for people, especially her siblings.

She had two brothers and one sister. Her sister's name was Kate, one of her brothers was Jake, and her other brother was Mike. Kate was seven years old, Jake was four, and Mike was three. JoJo was turning three years old herself, and she was sad because she had to celebrate her birthday without her parents.

"Here, I got you a present," Kate said. It was a big bug with 12 legs and was sticky—it looked like a fly.

When JoJo first saw the big bug, she was disgusted because it was bigger than her, but as she wrapped it in her web, it got smaller and smaller, like magic! The next day, JoJo was sleeping. Her brother, Mike, was trying to wake her up because it was the day they were going to rescue their mom and dad. Their mom and dad, Jessica and Bob, had been captured by the evil scientist Dr. James Martinez several months ago, because he wanted to become rich and famous by pretending to discover Tiger Spiders. But what Dr. Martinez did not know was that JoJo and Mike were going to trap him and get their parents back.

Mike screamed, "Wake up, JoJo!"

She woke up and mumbled, "What do you want? I am trying to sleep."

Mike apologized, "I am sorry, but today is the day we go get Mom and Dad. Are you ready?"

"Oh my God, for real? It is already the day? I can't believe the scientist fell for our trick!" exclaimed JoJo.

Mike said, "Let's go."

JoJo and Mike had tricked Dr. Martinez into meeting with them, because he thought the two Tiger Spiders were going to give him $13,000 to build a machine that would extract DNA from Bob and Jessica, so Dr. Martinez could clone more Tiger Spiders.

JoJo and Mike left their house, where they lived in the basement. They grabbed a map and were ready to go. JoJo and Mike walked through the sewers that they used to travel from their house. They had only walked a couple of blocks before JoJo began to get bored and tired.

"Are we there yet?" JoJo said in a tired voice.

Mike responded, "We are almost there, we just have 10 miles to go."

Ten miles passed, and JoJo became so tired of the smell and the darkness of the sewer that she and Mike crawled out of the nearest manhole. Luckily, they could see the house where Dr. Martinez lived.

When they saw the house, they thought it was going to be a science lab but it was a normal house. It was brown and it was big, but it didn't look creepy. It had tinted windows, though, so you couldn't see inside. JoJo and her brother both rang the doorbell. A guy came out who you would think was a normal guy, but he had his hair up, and had a lab coat and glasses. He had spiky hair, and looked nice (because he was always smiling). He beckoned JoJo and Mike inside.

"Yes, how can I help you?" said Dr. Martinez.

JoJo and Mike said, "We've got your money in our magic tiger-skin suitcase."

The scientist said, "Can I see the money?"

JoJo and Mike opened up the suitcase. While Dr. Martinez was distracted by the fake money they'd placed inside the case—*bang!* JoJo and Mike trapped the scientist with their webs and asked where their parents were.

The scientist said, "I will never tell you because I need my money."

ILLUSTRATOR: JAY FLECK / STUDENT: MIA TOLAYO, PAGE 33

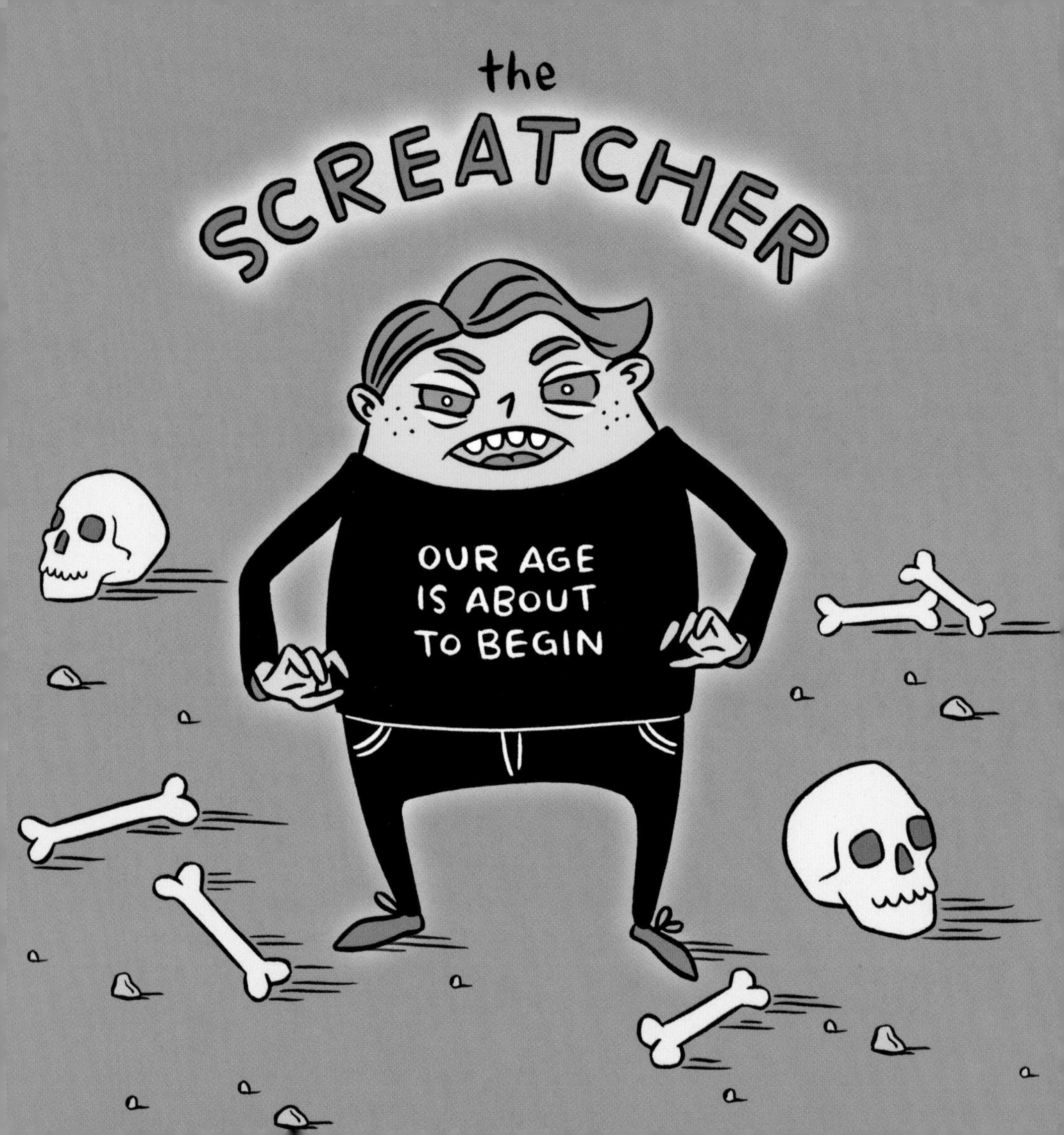
the SCREATCHER
OUR AGE IS ABOUT TO BEGIN

The two Tiger Spiders noticed that there was a closed door with seven separate locks on it. Thankfully, the scientist had forgotten to close it, since he hadn't expected betrayal. JoJo and Mike ran through the door and into the attic, which doubled as Dr. Martinez's workspace. The workspace was full of microscopes, tubes, and a giant machine connected to the chemicals that stored JoJo and Mike's parents. Dr. Martinez was using the machine to see if he could mutate the poor Tiger Spiders.

JoJo yelled, "There's Mom!"

"Mom! Dad!" said Mike and JoJo.

You might wonder how Mom and Dad got out. On top of the machine where they were being stored there was a blue circle with a password entry on it. Luckily, Dr. Martinez had written down the password since he didn't want to forget it. JoJo and Mike were able to punch in *D-R-.-M* and open the machine, freeing their parents. Afterwards, JoJo and Mike grabbed a rope, tied Dr. Martinez up even more, and threw him into the attic.

JoJo, Mike, Jessica, and Bob started walking home, back through the sewer to get to their house. Of course, they didn't walk through the stinky garbage water, since it was gross and wet. They walked along the ceiling to avoid touching the stinky water.

Once they got home, Jake and Kate were very excited to see their parents again, but Mike exclaimed, "What are we gonna do? That evil scientist is gonna get loose and come after us!"

JoJo responded, "You're right! I have a plan, though: We're going to go down to the sewers again, and we're going to live in there. Dr. James Martinez won't come after us because he only has one lab coat, and he doesn't want to wash it."

So the Tiger Spider family began to pack. They took some pictures of themselves when they were younger, their sofa, and their TV. They put everything in the beautiful tiger-skin suitcase they'd used to trick Dr. Martinez. JoJo, Mike, Kate, Jake, Jessica, and Bob began to walk toward the deepest, darkest part of the sewer, where they knew Dr. James Martinez wouldn't find them. They went to where the sewer got really nasty; everything was squishy and slimy. Everything there got stuck all over them and worst of all, it smelled like a dead rat that had been soaked in really stinky tea.

The Tiger Spider family opened their magic tiger-skin suitcase, but the minute they put down their family photos, TV, and sofa, it all sank into the muck.

"Oh my God! Our family photos and my TV! Gone!" exclaimed JoJo.

"No, that was my TV," argued Mike.

"Well, kids, at least we're all safe down here," Jessica said. What they didn't know was that Dr. Martinez had escaped from his attic and used a magnifying glass to find the footprints of the Tiger Spider family so he could capture all of them—not just their parents. When he found out they were in the darkest, deepest part of the sewer, he devised a plan: He coated his lab coat in armor so it wouldn't get messy, installed a brain widget so he could command his robotic coat with his mind, and put in a secret compartment full of tacos in case he got hungry.

Just as the Tiger Spider family was sitting down to a nice meal, Dr. Martinez busted in and said, "Ha! I caught you!"

At the same time, his robotic coat began to *beep* and *boop*, warning him that the water was growing deeper. As he walked toward the Tiger Spiders, he began to sink deeper into the stinky muck. By the time he reached JoJo and her family, only his head was above all the gross trash. His coat was too heavy to allow him to climb out of the mush and claim his prize.

"You might have gotten away with this," he gagged as the sewer smell filled his nostrils, "But I'll get you next time!"

Every member of the Tiger Spider family—JoJo, Mike, Jake, Kate, Jessica and Bob—all hopped on his head on the way out.

With Dr. Martinez out of the way, the Tiger Spiders went back to their old house, but now, instead of living down in the basement and in fear of the evil scientist, they moved into the house itself.

"Yay! Finally we're free!" they all said.

"But my TV is still gone," Jake said, sadly.

"Just forget it," JoJo said, relieved.

Dr. Martinez, after freeing himself of his robotic coat, got used to the stinky smells and squishy floors of the sewer and decided he kind of liked it. He just ended up staying there. "Science," he said, "is just too much of a hassle."

Eventually, JoJo and her family moved to a big house in the woods that was full of Tiger Spiders! As JoJo got older, the young Tiger Spiders would gather around and ask her to tell the story of how she saved her parents. She never refused.

Marvin and the Dream Monster

by MARVIN LAZO

n the year 1903, there lived a teenager named Nick who was 17 years old. He always had a dream to be king—a king of anything. But his parents told him he would never be a king. He was abused, doing their work and being their minion. He ran away, hoping he would never see them again.

He went to a city in Europe where there were a lot of spies. At that time, it was the beginning of World War I. This was the time when one spy tried to disappear a prince and his wife, and Nick happened to die, caught in the spy's drama.

MAY 30, 2015, 4:36 PM

An 11-year-old kid called Marvin Lazo was doing a project on World War I and wanted to take a nap, so he did. When he dreamt, the teen who died came into Marvin's dream!

"Hi, my name is Nick. Nick Dickson."

"Wait, the teen who died, right?" Marvin asked.

"Yup, that's me," replied Nick.

"I feel sad for you," Marvin sighed.

"Thanks. Where am I?" asked Nick.

"My dream. Why?" Marvin gasped.

"Oh. You can do anything in dreams, right?" smiled Nick.

"Yeah, mostly," Marvin replied.

"So, did you know I'm going to destroy everyone's dream?" laughed Nick. He summoned a fortune cookie. Marvin quickly caught it and read, *You have met a terrible fate.*

"Mike and Sarah!" shouted Marvin when he woke up.

"What happened?" Sarah asked curiously.

"Wait, where's Mike?" asked Marvin.

"He's sleeping," said Sarah.

"No!" shouted Marvin.

"What?" asked Sarah.

"The reason there have recently been so many disappearances is because a monster goes into people's dreams and tries to kidnap them!" shouted Marvin.

"Wait, what?!" Sarah screamed.

Marvin ran to Mike's bedroom door.

"NO NO NO NO NO NO NO! He's gone. Mike is gone," cried Sarah.

Marvin heard an evil voice. The same voice that he had heard in the dream realm.

"It was you. *You* made Mike disappear," Marvin said to Nick, furiously.

"Yes, it was me, and it was fun. I have to go. Bye."

"Wait, no!" Marvin said, but then fainted.

"Marvin! Marvin! Marvin!" screamed Sarah.

Marvin woke up, and he was confused.

"I need to talk to your brother, Jeff," said Marvin.

"Jeff, I need to talk to you," said Marvin.

"I know, Marvin. Sarah told me everything. I found a way to get into our dreams and stop Nick."

"Then let's go!" said Marvin.

"Marvin, wait! Not yet," Jeff said. "If we disappear in the dream realm, we disappear in real life."

"No matter what, we still are doing it," Marvin said. "Now let's go."

"We should have a team name," Jeff said. "What should it be, Marvin?"

"*The Losers*," Marvin responded.

"Marvin, you're already a loser," Jeff remarked.

"Shut up, we're here," Marvin said. Nick was standing right in front of them.

"Well, you came," Nick said. "Let's fight! But call me The Screatcher now."

"Wait . . . you changed your name?"

"Yup. It's scarier, and no one's name is The Screatcher," Nick/The Screatcher responded.

Marvin grabbed a purple bubble gun and an epic fight began. Marvin and Jeff made a shelter and tried fighting, but Mike, who was under The Screatcher's control, summoned an army.

The Screatcher teleported behind Marvin and bit Jeff with his teeth.

"Why are you doing this?" Marvin asked The Screatcher.

"Because I always wanted to be a king," The Screatcher responded. "And being in peoples' dreams will let them know I'm king. I enter their brains to control."

"Why not just be a king in *your* dream?" Marvin suggested.

The Screatcher paused for a moment. "You're right. I should have done that instead."

Marvin teleported behind The Screatcher and said, "Sorry, but this is for Mike and Jeff everyone else you disappeared."

Shouting angrily, he trapped The Screatcher in a water jail, where he fell asleep for five years.

Just then, Jeff, Mike, and all the people who were disappeared by him came back from the dream realm—the dream powers of The Screatcher disappeared when he was caught.

MARCH 9TH, 2020 1:09 PM

"This ice cream is fantastic!" shouted Marvin.

"You've said it!" echoed Jeff. "Marvin, you know about The Screatcher, right?" asked Jeff.

"Yeah. Why?"

"It's been five years. He's about to come out of jail, so watch out!" warned Jeff.

"I see," replied Marvin.

Back in the dream realm, The Screatcher was plotting. "I'm free finally, but they know my secret, so I must create an army," he said.

"Come out of the dream realm and go to Earth, Master!" yelled a minion in the dream realm.

"Our age is about to begin!" declared The Screatcher.

Tim's Revenge

by ALEXIS CORRAL

O nce, there was a type of species from another dimension, on an unknown planet that was red, yellow, and very tiny. They saw a human scientist named Brian taking over their planet. He was a 28-year-old male; size 5.2 feet with red eyes, black hair, no mustache, and a tiny beard.

When Brian the scientist was done with his job, he took off and didn't suspect the creature following behind him. The floating creature was two feet tall and had white eyes and blue skin. His name was Tim, and he had powers like water, fire, wind, teleportation, and Earth. He had tiny, water bottle arms, was seven years old, and looked like blue fire floating without legs.

Tim followed the scientist on his way back to Earth. The little creature had never seen such a marvelous world with so many living creatures and humans. He was hungry, until he saw a restaurant full of food and snuck inside it.

Tim was devouring all the pies in the dessert section until the chef caught him eating. He ran in a flash. Tim saw a garbage can and hid for about five years. When he came out of the garbage can, Tim saw some things change. He saw Obama. He came to the White House to meet him, but not everyone could see Tim's type of species. It's like they're invisible to unworthy people, like when Tim was trying to meet Obama.

Tim went to a random kid's house and he frightened a little baby boy. Some mysterious people whispered together, "What is wrong with the baby?" because they were curious. Tim was also curious about why the baby was sobbing, so he tried to discover the reason. The Leader rocked the baby, until he went back to sleep.

ILLUSTRATOR: TJ KISER / STUDENT: SUNNIVA ROTHEIM, PAGE 53

Tim whispered, "Who are you people?"

The Leader responded, "We are the guardians of this planet. This is John, and this is Mindy, also Clare, and last but not least, me, Drake. We came here to help you with your problem—your species are being captured by a scientist named Brian."

They made a deal. If the Guardians helped Tim and his species, then Tim would help them rebuild their teleporter, which was broken.

At first, their plan failed. Well, they were just running around with no plan at all. Tim's friends were blaming each other because they lost. They started to fight. Tim yelled, "Even though we lost the battle, there's no need to fight!"

The Guardians all echoed, "You're right. We're just wasting our time!"

The Guardians and Tim's species tried again, this time with a plan. Their plan was that Tim would be bait, and the Guardians would steal a remote control button from the evil scientist, Brian, by building machines that were backpacks with robotic arms coming out of them. These machines would allow the Guardians to fly and be invisible. The invisibility would let them pass through security, and the flying ability would be so powerful that Brian the scientist wouldn't be able to catch them and the camera couldn't even record them.

They actually did the plan, and it worked! While Brian was chasing Tim, Brian noticed that the remote control button was gone. He went back to his laboratory to look, but Brian couldn't find it.

Tim went back to the Guardians of the Earth, who were hanging out on top of the ceiling in Brian's laboratory, where they captured Brian and freed the species of Tim.

Tim said, "Thank you."

The Guardians responded, "You're welcome."

Tim fixed the Guardians' teleporter, and they all went back to their worlds, living happy and free.

Tom and Mary's Life

by ROSA ARTEAGA

here was a beastly monster girl named Mary who had a boyfriend named Tom. Tom was a monster as well. They lived in a red, sparkly house with a blue roof. The door was green. They lived downtown in a quick and quiet place. They moved there because they had heard it was very peaceful. Mary was 16 years old and Tom was 18 years old. They had moved in together on October 13th, back when Mary was 13 and Tom was 15, which is when they started dating each other.

How did they meet?

Mary had no friends until Tom walked by and asked, "Are you OK?"

Mary looked up and said, "Yes, I'm OK. Can I run away with you?"

Tom replied, "OK."

Since then, they've been dating for fun.

Every night at sundown, Tom and Mary usually go to the woods. One time, Tom said, "Look over there!"

Wolves started to look at the moon.

Tom took her home and told Mary, "I can't date you any more." Tom had lost the spark for Mary.

Mary said, "OK." Mary didn't care anymore.

Tom was so disappointed that candy corn came out of his eyes instead of tears. He thought Mary didn't like him any more, even though he was the one who ended it with *her*. They stopped dating for a little bit, but they still texted each other and talked to each other on the phone.

Tom would say, "Hi."

Mary would madly reply, "Hi."

On New Year's Eve, they went outside and tried to find each other, but then they both thought to go to the park where they first met. It was midnight. At the same time, they both yelled, "Hi!"

"I miss you," Tom said.

"Same," said Mary.

Tom said to Mary, "Can we be friends?"

Mary said, "Yes. I would like that."

At the same time they said, "We are BFF's forever. Let's have a party."

Tom and Mary looked at each other and both screamed, "YES!"

They decorated the house and asked all of their friends to come. They told them that there would be chocolate cake. All of their friends arrived. They had picked up ice cream on the way.

At the end, Mary told Tom that she had an awesome time. All of their friends went home to do more sleeping.

The Story of the Wrecked Arm

by VIOLETA PEREZ

urpuly is 15 years old and lives near a very sandy beach located on Wilton Street. Purpuly's house is oval, the outside is painted lavender, and the inside wallpaper is tan. In the winter, it never gets cold because it stays as warm as a teddy bear in a baby's crib. She sleeps in a closet filled with hot and cozy blankets. Purpuly has long, pretty, flowing hair and is furry, blue-eyed, and five feet tall, with short feet. She was born in a dark cave with webs everywhere. Her insides are caring like a bunny, sweet as a candy bar, and nice like a baby.

Purpuly's superpowers are to cook fast, clean fast, shop fast, and she has superspeed in general. She has a squeaky voice, like an old wooden door in a creepy haunted house that also sounds cute. She likes to sing, dance, shop, and watch TV. She drives her blue Lokana car to go to work. Her dream is to have a mansion with a water slide that is orange, because she likes the color orange. She is afraid of spiders. Her secret is that she loves books, but she tells people that she hates books.

Purpuly loves tuna sandwiches and eats them a lot for lunch. One day, she was going shopping for tuna, bread, and orange juice at Jewel. She went to the canned food section and got the tuna, then went to the bread section to get her white bread . . . but it was too high up to reach.

"Can you give me the bread up there?" she asked an employee. The employee got a ladder for Purpuly to reach.

Purpuly smiled and screamed out loud, "Thank you!"

She went to the juice section and got three orange juices. Purpuly went to the cashier and got out her credit card from her blue purse. She swiped her card down, then she entered her PIN. She put her food and drinks in a big brown bag. She came out of the store with a yellow cart and went to the parking lot, looking for her blue car. Purpuly backed up the car slowly and drove out of the parking lot.

She was driving to her oval house at the beach when all of a sudden a person named Nanu—a monster who loves to go outside to play or shop at stores—hit Purpuly's blue car with her precious, brand new, pink car!

Purpuly tried to get out of her car but her arm was broken like a wrecked ball. She screamed out, "My arm, my arm!"

Another person ran out of their car to help Purpuly get out.

That person also called the ambulance for help.

"Hello, um, I need an ambulance on Elmer Street!"

Nanu and Purpuly got into an argument.

Purpuly's cousin came from cold Canada later that day. They took her home after she came out of the hospital.

"You are OK. Breathe in and out, Purpuly," said her mother.

"OK," she said, in a sad mood. Her arm was in pain.

Her family came to see her broken arm. Some of her cousins were British and Italian. They were going to stay with her because she could not do a lot of stuff like cook or clean and write letters. Her family went to the hospital to check on Purpuly's arm.

"Please help my daughter, please," whispered her mom.

Purpuly went to Nanu's house to talk about the car accident. Then they went to Rock'in Coffee to get coffee and donuts. They talked about what happened.

Nanu said, "I am sorry that I crashed into you. I was feeling dizzy and I am mad at you also, because it was my brand new car that I got at Cars Are Me."

Purpuly said, "It's OK it happened, but my arm is still hurting. My cast will help, the doctors said."

Nanu said, "Let's have a party and let's be friends."

"OK," said Purpuly.

Purpuly had a party at Purpuly's house and Nanu and Purpuly became friends. They had chips, pop, pizza, and cupcakes. They had a dance-off and Purpuly's cousin won.

Quest for the Good Suit

by SUNNIVA ROTHEIM

Once upon a time, a little baby was born. She had long, black hair, her skin was white as snow, and her eyes were as red as the Devil. Her name was Dece. Her mother's name was Kin O'Dark, and she always told Dece that one day they would take over the world. They would be evil forever.

Dece lived in a black-and-white house next to the monster park in Monstrousa. When Dece turned six, she started at Monstrano School where she made a friend named Lilusa.

Lilusa had long, pretty white hair. Her skin was green, and her eyes were as blue as the sea. Her grandfather was King Light Flower. Lilusa lived with him because her parents were dead. Dece and Lilusa became best friends.

When Dece and Lilusa turned 15 years old, a dark shadow showed up and shouted like it was important, "One day, you two will have a significant thing to do!"

One dark night, Kin O'Dark hypnotized the guards at the castle and captured King Light Flower. She put the king in the dungeon. The hypnosis could only be broken if somebody captured Kin O'Dark and put her in the dungeon, too, where her powers would be lost. Kin O'Dark tried to find and destroy the "Good Suit," which could be used to capture her.

Dece wanted to help Lilusa find the "Good Suit" and capture Kin O'Dark. She wanted to free all the people and make the world a safe place.

Kin O'Dark had spies who knew what Lilusa and Dece were doing. She was furious when she heard that her daughter was helping the king. She was doing everything she could to find her daughter and Dece and put them in the dungeons, too.

Kin O'Dark was torturing the guards to tell her where the "Good Suit" was, but no guards knew where it was hidden. Lilusa had been told that the "Good Suit" was hidden in the forest inside a big tree with a secret door. This door opened with a special command that Lilusa knew.

Lilusa and Dece found the tree where the "Good Suit" was hidden. The spies were getting closer, though, so the girls had to hurry before they were captured. The girls were able to open the door in the tree and find the suit.

Lilusa and Dece escaped the woods and fought their way towards the castle. When they arrived, Dece put on the "Good Suit" and put a spell on Kin O'Dark. They took her to the dungeon and locked her up. The guards' hypnosis was broken, and they started acting normally again. King Light Flower then took power and everyone lived in a safe world again.

Back to Boonville High School

by EMILY MONRREAL

nce a upon a time, there was a monster named Jeff. He was not just any ordinary monster but a smart monster—nice and imaginative, too. When he was little he said his first words: "Mommy" and "Daddy," but now he is 19 years old and loved school. He was ready for high school. He lived in a fancy home and his room was in the basement. Jeff was very nice, careful, and super speedy for gym on track day.

Jeff made fart sounds, ran a lot, and moved around a lot in his car (a Pagani Huayra, $1.3 million). When he got home, he would go in the backyard and play with his monster friends, Gabriel and Estevan. They were the landlord's kids, and they played together a lot. One had been in school, and one was just starting school. Estevan was three and loved Jeff as a friend, and Gabriel, too. Their parents were Dulce and Cody.

Jeff's fear was to get detention. He was also afraid of spiders, snakes, mad teachers, angry moms, and disappointed dads. His dream was to get straight A's on his report card. His parents said he had good habits. He loved his teachers and hated bullies. He also hated that his superspeed powers were getting him super tired. Jeff relaxed by going to Boo Beach to get a tan. Whenever it rained, the rain didn't go there because there was a remote that closed the roof. It was more like an indoor pool, but there was still sand for sandcastles.

One day, he made his first monster bid—like a Facebook page but just for monsters. Jeff was in his room packing up clothes for gym on his first day of high school, and Jeff's little brother, Matt, took his math and reading notebook.

Matt said, "You're gonna get in trouble on the first day of school." Matt said that he'd be in trouble because he liked to do that to all three of his brothers: Jeff, Eli, and Armani.

Jeff ran to Matt's room to find his notebook, took it back, and put it in his bookbag. His mother, Alanda, called for breakfast. It was waffles with orange juice.

Alanda said, "Get in the car so you won't be late for high school."

When he got there, the bell rang and all the kids ran from the bully except for Jeff. Jeff walked up and saw two kids with their heads down making crying noises.

It was a trick.

The two bullies raised their heads and yelled, "Go!"

The third bully grabbed Jeff and put him in the trash.

He met his first slip to detention on his first day, and Principal Willie said loudly, "Why are you not in class? Here's a slip to detention."

Jeff sadly asked, "But why?"

"You know you did not go to class. Good day, sir." The two sad kids were bullies who were getting new kids in trouble. Jeff asked if he could call his mother, and she asked what happened.

Jeff was crying and said, "I'm in detention."

Alanda got mad and wanted to have a meeting. When they were all there with the bully, he didn't like the hat Jeff had on, so he put him in the trash can.

When he got his report card, Jeff had straight A's. So he got his second car, which is another Pagani Huayra, which costs $1.3 million again, because his first car broke.

So he drove to Vladland to find agent Vladimir. Agent Vladimir took him to Glow Chicken Island, and Jeff touched five chickens to get the power of punching. Then he went and told agent Vladimir to take him back to school so he could defeat the bully with one punch, but not a hard punch.

He just did it like a pinch, and told him not to bully anyone, because it could affect your grades.

He saw the bully with the principal, who told Edwards, "Edwards Junior, you are expelled. I'll see you tomorrow by your locker."

So when Principal Willie said, "Good day, sir," Jeff hid in his locker.

Principal Willie turned around and left. So Jeff got out of the locker and punched Edwards softly on the arm and became best friends with the other bullies, too. They were really nice. And Gabriel and Estevan became friends with them, too.

They went off to science class to stop the punching powers, but Jeff brought Gabriel and Estevan to help, because they were smart. So Gabriel and Estevan gave Jeff a *Stop My Power* potion.

He drank it and ran to the bus, screaming, "Stop the bus!" And he got on and went home. Jeff thought he should go to bed.

"Goodnight, Mom!" he said, and fell asleep.

The next day, Jeff screamed, "GOOD MORNING, MOM!"

He did not hear a response from Mom that morning, or the night before, so he went downstairs to look for his mom and saw a note that said, *I locked your mom up in a cage. You can never find her*.

Jeff used his magic spell book to get his powers back. Then he went to get his mom, and the evil man froze her. He couldn't touch her, but he had a potion to stop everything.

He threw it at his mom, and his mom unfroze!

Smelly Socks, Old Toys, and Another Dimension: Things I Found Under My Bed!

by KAYLA SANTIAGO

 monster was born in another world.

One day, I, Kayla, went upstairs and went on my computer. Then my mom told me to clean my room, so I got off the computer. I went under my bed and saw a small door. I opened the door and saw another planet. I closed the door and I was confronted by a monster. Her name was Nicky. She had blue eyes, soft brown fur, and she wasn't scared of me. We started to talk.

"Hi Kayla!" said Nicky.

"Hi," I said.

"Kayla, I have to tell you something. I lost my parents."

"I can help you find them," I said.

"I'm so happy you will help me find them!"

We became friends. She told me the story of her life. She was named after a princess on her planet who died a long time ago. When Nicky was a baby, her parents gave her a ruby locket, and she cherished this locket for the rest of her life. Nicky also told me how another monster named Napo separated her from her parents. Napo was a jealous monster with black fur and red eyes, and he made weird humming sounds. When he hummed, thousands of soldiers would appear and use their superpowers to trap people in caves that were found all over the planet. He didn't like Nicky's dad or mom.

Nicky lost her parents the year she was born. Napo actually took her parents one day when they were in the kitchen making baby food for Nicky. They were preparing *pomogwini*, which is a monster food that has green seeds in it and it makes you wake up in the morning.

Now, Nicky wanted to know more about them. Who were her real parents? She had taken care of herself all these years and she had a flashback of when she was a baby, how her parents took care of her. She saw in her monster mind how they fed her and she learned to do that for herself.

To look for her parents, Nicky and I first looked in a cave. It was really dark and there was a little door that only opens when it's dark. It was hot in there, but then it started cooling down. We went to see what was behind the door. Nicky started to see a different flashback about her parents in her mind. She saw a moment in her mind when her monster mom was holding her as a baby. I saw the look on Nicky's face. She was a little shocked, by the way. Then she saw that her parents were stuck somewhere and she needed to go help them. But we didn't find them in the cave.

Next, we looked in the door under my bed, and it was awesome. We kept going on a path and then there was a black house with three monsters standing outside, all soldiers in Napo's army. Nicky recognized them, but since she had powers, she could turn herself invisible and she turned me invisible, too.

We went inside the house, and it was scary and creepy. There were rats running everywhere, hiding from Napo. There was a cage that other monsters were in, so we tried to help them escape. We snuck by the cage and all of a sudden Nicky had another flashback where she remembered where Napo kept his keys! He kept them in a dungeon in the basement.

First, we went to the dungeon and found his keys in a little box where Nicky had to say a password and she opened it. Then, we went upstairs and we found her parents. They were stuck on a metal bed and we got them unstuck. We actually found Napo's tools and were able to take apart the bed frame. Their bodies were tilted, by the way, curved into the shape of the bed. They had been lying in the bed for over a 100 years. Their fur was brown and white, hardened by time. I met her parents and they were happy that I had saved them. They thanked me for bringing back Nicky and for helping them get free from Napo's grip.

After Nicky found her parents, they gave her a special potion for me to drink so that I could return to my normal self. She also left the door open under my bed so that I could visit her any time.

I went back home and started cleaning my room, thinking a lot about Nicky. I will always remember her because she was kind of like me, and we kind of liked the same things, like playing games, finding information on the computer, and playing basketball. Where Nicky lives, it sounds like an amazing planet, and I would like to visit her again.

Nicky went home with her parents, and the ruby locket that she wore around her neck turned into another dimension so that they could return to their planet.

I never saw Nicky again, but I know that the door is always open.

The Rise of the Hero

by LEODAN VENEGAS

Shadow was born on a very boring and dark planet. Now, Shadow lives and sleeps in a fluffy cloud and collects bananas. Shadow is a shadow with all human abilities. He also has teleportation as a power and wears a brown cape. Shadow is secretive, stealthy, and brave. Shadow can teleport into movies, books, and all dimensions. He talks in a normal way and tries not to sound scary. He dreams to rule everything created, especially bananas. He's scared of light but he loves bananas, as well as catching bananas and other objects. He likes his master, Tiko, who is a small ninja trainer. He relaxes in a Jacuzzi and likes to play dimension tag with his friends. Dimension tag is tag around any dimension, so you teleport and tag.

Shadow thinks he's going to become the world's biggest hero and wants to be the leader of the banana tribe, which is basically his family. Shadow usually goes to different dimensions to get banana plants or seeds because he gets stronger by collecting bananas. If he's weak, it's because he doesn't have enough bananas.

One day, Shadow was at his house and chilling. He was relaxing and swimming in a Jacuzzi when suddenly, a gigantic meteor fell. This meteor was massive. It could break houses or trees.

"Ahhhh!" screamed Shadow.

He followed the meteor. "Oh, man." He got closer. "Wh-what's happening?"

Then, Shadow teleported to Crash Landing, where the meteor came from. Crash Landing is an old smashed up land with cannons that launch boulders. It is like an old construction world. There, he saw Cromis, the Launching King.

I LOVE CATCHING BANANAS

61

"Why did you send the meteors?" asked Shadow. The world was shaking. "What was that?"

"You fool," yelled Cromis. "You unbalanced the galaxy. We're all going to die."

"No, we're not. I have super powers. CALM DOWN!" yelled Shadow.

The Islands were going to explode. The Islands are the neighbors who live in clouds. But the Islands made Earth so dangerous that pieces of Earth started falling apart! The world was in danger, so Shadow mashed up the canons and made a gigantic cannon and shot a massive meteor. Then, they put clouds around the meteors so they would not damage the Earth. They sent meteors to make Earth whole again.

"I hope it works."

"On three. One, two, three."

"What happened?"

It worked. The world came back to life. Humans danced in circles. The world was happy. The cloud was upgraded into a mansion. It was the happiest day ever. Everyone shouted so loud the cheers of joy went to outer space. After the galaxy quake, Shadow talked to Cromis.

"Sorry for stopping you from sending meteors."

"It's OK," said Cromis.

BEEP. The planet moved to the other side. Crash Landing shook and moved off to the other side of Earth.

"OK, come on. We've got a job to do!" yelled the king, Cromis.

From that day on, Shadow lived in peace and Cromis kept sending the meteors for fun. And any time Cromis would go to the cloud, he would get Shadow to help him build a new home.

ILLUSTRATOR: ASHLEY ELANDER / STUDENT: EMILY DRZEWIECKI, PAGE 65

Tsunami the Big Blue Fish

by EMILY DRZEWIECKI

ILLUSTRATOR: JEFFREY BROWN / STUDENT: BRIELLE BERRY, PAGE 68

 ne day by a town, there was an ocean. At the bottom of that ocean floor there was a tiny fish named Blue. His name was Blue because he was a blue fish who wanted to be a person.

A few days later, something happened. A scientist on his speedboat threw toxic waste into the ocean. The toxic waste was bright green. It went down deep to the ocean floor and exploded on Blue's home. His home was destroyed.

Blue was affected by the toxic waste and grew bigger and bigger until he fell under the ocean floor. He was as big as the ocean and heavier than the water that he fell under.

Of course, he was OK with it at first. He thought the effects would go away. But two weeks later, he got as mad as a bull because he felt alone with no friends and was very hungry. He shook the bottom floor with his tail and created a big wave, bigger than any other wave the townsfolk had seen before! The town saw it and was very alert about it.

The town was a small town and had very few houses. It was close to the ocean and everyone loved the ocean. It was always colorful when the sun went down with all the colorful lights. Everyone knew each other and they were all friends.

The whole town went to hide in their basements and they were hoping the big wave would pass, but it didn't.

Water was coming down the basement stairs, making big floods in the basements. The flood was rising higher and higher. It got to be as high as a giraffe.

In one basement in one part of town, a random dad called out, "What's happening?"

A random mom answered, "I don't know!"

Their kid cried out, "I'm scared!"

The mom answered, "It's OK, we all are!" She hugged the child.

They hid in the bathroom in their basement, so not as much water could get to them. They all felt so scared and terrified thinking about what was going to happen.

In another basement in another part of town, a guy spoke to his friend. "Dude, what's going on?"

His friend replied, "I don't know!"

The guy whined, "Oh no!"

They both yelled at the same time, "A FLOOD!"

Two hours later, the flooding stopped and everyone went outside. The town was destroyed. It looked like there had been an elephant stampede and the whole town was silent. That day, the giant fish Blue also became called Tsunami. Tsunami means a very big wave.

Tsunami is 100 years old. Every full moon he would make another gigantic wave. Tsunami was all alone in the dark, under the bottom of the ocean floor. The townspeople wanted to know what made these big waves because they did not know that Blue made the waves. There were scientists who were in a science lab, looking for research about the tsunami.

The research did not help and they had to dig deeper. So they tried to make toxic waste again and yeah—they made the tsunami. They tossed it into the ocean down under to the bottom of the ocean. The toxic waste reached the big fish and he turned into . . . you guessed it. Tsunami's dream: being a person!

Tsunami swam to the top of the ocean. He felt awesome at first and when he reached the top, he was out of breath. Tsunami said, "Wow, I feel so weird and awful. Being a human is terrible. I need to find the lab that made the toxic waste that made me human."

Back on land, behind the long trees, Tsunami looked behind him and saw a big board that said: *THE ONLY SCIENCE LAB IN TOWN.*

Now, he knew where to go because right before he turned human in the explosion, he read the label on the big metal can that was holding the toxic waste. It said *Made By The Scientists* on it.

At night, he broke into the lab, but it was hard for him to walk because he had never used human legs before and his legs were like noodles. He got to the lab by following the board.

Inside the lab were all the colorful liquids—pink, blue, and even glow-in-the-dark liquids. He combined the liquids together. He poured them into one big glass. Then he made three liquids.

He drank the first thin liquid and it tasted like magic, but nothing happened.

Next, he drank the second liquid and it was thick and boiling, like lava, but nothing happened.

Last but not least, he drank the third one and it was slushy and as cold as an iceberg. Still nothing happened.

Tsunami was really calm because he had to make one more perfect liquid. He made it using blue, red, green, purple, pink, black, orange, and white liquids. The liquid was bubbling and it was a color that was never seen before. It was more beautiful than a rainbow butterfly.

Then, he went to the ocean because he knew fish can't breathe air. When he got to the ocean he drank the liquid.

Then he turned into a fish! And there was never a tsunami again.

But he kept the name.

The Amazing Gerald's Life Story

by BRIELLE LEILANI BERRY

here once was a family of sheep. Their mom had just had her third baby, but that baby wasn't like the other ones. That baby was half-human, half-sheep! They named him Gerald. Gerald was very soft, smart, and kind. Gerald was very small, had four legs, two arms, the body of a sheep, and the head of a human. They took care of Gerald for a while, but then they got really embarrassed because the other sheep kept staring at them. One day, while Gerald was sleeping, the family left him.

Gerald started to grow up and found a strange place that was something like a house in a cave. It had been abandoned for years. When Gerald stepped inside the house, he realized everything was made out of grass.

Gerald asked this strange thing (a human), "Why is the house full of grass?" But when Gerald tried to talk, he could only yell, "Baaa!"

The man had no idea what Gerald was saying, so he told Gerald to write it. The man gave Gerald an Expo marker and dry-erase board. Gerald wrote, *Why is this house full of grass?*

The man answered, "The house used to belong to a man named Jayden who had the chicken pox, so he used special grass and glue so he would never have to water it. He did this so he could use the grass to scratch himself."

That's cool, Gerald wrote.

The man told Gerald that his name was Oscar. When Oscar finished telling the story, Gerald went into the house and made himself comfortable. Gerald's stomach growled.

Grrrrrrr. Gerald tried a piece of the grass and it tasted horrible. He didn't even like regular grass! What was he thinking?

Oscar asked Gerald, "Do you want to go grab a bite?"

Yes, Gerald wrote.

They decided to go to the Anything You Can Eat World! You can literally eat anything you want! All you have to do is say what you want to eat and the people will make it!

Gerald and Oscar decided to order the Crazy Sandwich. Gerald's Crazy Sandwich had a cut banana, pickles, spaghetti, mashed potatoes, and butter. Oscar ordered the exact same thing, but with different secret toppings. Everyone gasped because of how Gerald looked.

Oscar and Gerald decided to eat their Crazy Sandwiches at Oscar's place, outside of the house but inside the cave. Gerald and Oscar didn't really talk about anything, but Gerald did write, *My sandwich is crazier because it has chocolate on it.*

Oscar announced, "I have an even crazier thing on my sandwich . . . wheatgrass!"

When they finished eating, Oscar left and Gerald went to bed.

The next day, Gerald had a plan to make everyone like him. The plan was to make a fake kid out of ham, spaghetti, chicken bones, googly eyes, and clothes. Gerald was going to put the kid in a tree and lure everyone by saying that there was a gum tree. Gerald knew everyone would want to taste the gum and see if it was different than regular gum. When the decoy/ fake kid fell, Gerald would catch it, and everyone would like him.

Gerald practiced and kept trying to catch the fake kid, but he couldn't.

"Ready or not, it's time," Gerald told himself as he lured everyone to the gum tree.

When everyone got there, there was actually a *real* kid falling from the tree! And Gerald caught him!

Everyone started clapping.

Then, when Gerald started to say something, he was actually able to say it! "Thank you, thank you," he said.

It turns out the kid who fell was named José, and he was the sheriff's son. José was tall and had black hair and brown eyes. José got grounded because he knew that he was not supposed to climb trees. When Gerald caught José, José was scared of Gerald's beastly looks. But then he was glad that Gerald had caught him.

Gerald started to talk because Mother Nature gifted him the ability to talk. Mother Nature is the spirit of Earth. Because he was such a good boy and had caught José, Gerald was now a superhero who Mother Nature had gifted with even more powers. Gerald's superpowers included flying, superstrength, heat vision, and mind-reading.

Most of all, Gerald was happy because he could talk. He announced things like, "You guys should have trusted me," and "It's going to take a lot of time for me to forgive you."

Oh! I almost forgot. Gerald's family found out what happened and they loved him.

The Different One

by JOANA REYES

 nce there were three different birds that were unlike any other kind. They were seven feet tall. One kind was from a strawberry. These birds were called the Red Big eaters. The second type was from a blueberry. They were called the Good Bluebirds. Last but not least were the purple birds that came from grapes. They were called the Big Purple Eaters. They were considered hideous, mean and without feelings. They were nasty and ugly because that was their personality; they had no reason to be mean and hideous.

But there was one Big Purple Eater that was different from the others. His name was Joshua. He was nasty and ugly, but he had feelings. He felt lonely because he had no friends. He would feel left out and desperate for friends. He was judged by different people, and that made him feel upset. Also, other Big Purple Eaters judged him. People and birds bullied him for being different. Nobody cared about him. Nobody understood him.

Making friends with differently colored big birds wasn't allowed because it would be considered a betrayal to his kind, and if he betrayed them, he would get a strike and a punishment. He tried to make friends with different colored big birds anyway by going to visit their park. He even moved to their school.

Joshua made a Bluebird friend. Bluebirds were supposed to be nice even though people were mean to them. He met his friend in the park and started talking—but remember, Joshua is still selfish and mean.

The Bluebird was a female. Her name was Denisa. She was the most beautiful bird in the history of birds. What made her beautiful was her personality and her physical beauty. She had a couple of friends and three siblings—two sisters and one brother. The youngest sister was named Brianna, the middle sister was Nicole and the brother's name was Marco. The oldest sister, Denisa, was in between Nicole and Marco. Denisa was sweet, kind, nice, brave, honest, and polite.

Joshua's first words to Denisa were, "Whoa, you're so beautiful!" which he said dumbly.

Joshua had feelings for Denisa and Joshua would go spend time with her and sometimes with Denisa's siblings. They went to movie premieres!

Pause!

This might sound crazy, but they're like humans. They do activities like going to movie premieres, swimming, and going to school.

Un-pause.

When I said they go to school, they're freshmen in Hutchins High School. Joshua wanted to study to be a construction worker. Denisa didn't know whether she wanted to be a teacher or a doctor.

When they got out of school, they all met in the park for an hour to finish algebra and science. The park didn't have any playgrounds. It had benches and it was mostly for big kids—like teens. They had one science project: to make a potion that changed something into something else, like an ant into a dog. Denisa and Joshua were partners. The project was due in a week. Joshua was an expert in science.

There was also going to be a bird festival for the three bird types: Red, Blue, and Purple. The birds didn't like each other, but each year there was a history celebration where all three types of birds gathered and tried to talk to each other. I know they're supposed to be mean to each other, but that's how it was.

A messenger told the king that Joshua had plenty of Bluebird friends. The messengers were some people that the king elected to tell him what was going on with the birds. Each bird had another bird with them to tell the king what they were doing.

The king made the rules and watched whoever broke the laws or rules. The king was angry and demanded, "Joshua has to pay for what he's done."

This was strike one, so Joshua had to make a lot of food for the festival. He had to make 1,000 plates of soup, 500 salad bowls, and 2,000 drinks. He also had to plan everything, and it had better be the best festival. He had one week and three days with three people to help him, but he also had the science fair project.

His helpers were Denisa, Nicole, and Brianna. Denisa planned to do the science fair project now and then plan the festival afterwards. They finished the potion. They used a dog as an example, so the dog turned into a cat. They were going to put the antidote in the dog's water and food, and there was nothing else on Earth that could change it back. After they made a lot of the antidote, they focused on the festival to complete.

They went and got all the ingredients for the soup and limes to make lime juice. The lime juice looked like the potion, so Brianna put the potion in the drinks because she was rushing.

Then all five of them—Joshua, Denisa, Nicole, Brianna, and Marco—went to Mills Mall. They went to get outfits for the festival and the night went really quick. Then it was the day of the festival and the science project was due. First, they went to present their project and they used the dog I was telling you about. Their score was 99%, an A+, so they went home early to start putting together drinks and to make sure the antidote was in every drink.

There were two hours left before the festival. Just when they were getting ready, *poof!* They became humans. Denisa went to get her hair and makeup done in a salon and then went home. She wore a really, really pretty dress, jewelry, and her high heels. Joshua put on his vest and shoes. It was the first time the festival was on and people started drinking and turning into humans. Even King Marco turned into one and their lives changed. They had beautiful houses and Joshua had a mansion. The mansions came from the king. Marco was really rich and got everyone a bird. The king had one, too.

Three years passed, and when Joshua asked Denisa to prom and she said, "Yes."

Now we're pausing and going to talk about the siblings. Nicole had two dogs, Coco and Balto, a girl and a boy. Coco had seven babies, two boys and five girls named Luna, Athena, Leila, Persephone, Spike, Tucker, and the youngest one, Josie. Joshua and Denisa are a couple, but if you're thinking that it ends there it doesn't.

Denisa was now 20 and Joshua was 21. I know that you're supposed to start and end high school, but in the bird world it was really different when you're 15 to 18.

The birds pressured Joshua to make an antidote so they could go back to normal. Joshua kept saying, "You can't go back to normal."

King Marco replied, "If you don't find an antidote you will go to prison."

But wait! What I didn't tell you is that it was April 1st and Joshua got so scared that he didn't eat. He transferred schools to try to make an antidote. He transferred to the best math and science academy.

At the school, there were a lot of bullies, especially Brendon Rubio. He was the biggest bully of them all. When Brendon saw Joshua walking he'd say, "You're a skeleton. You're not going to get around here."

Joshua didn't care. He went to talk to the science and math teacher, Mr. Reyes, the best science and math teacher ever. Joshua asked, "Is there an antidote that can turn something or someone back to normal?" Joshua explained the whole long story.

Mr. Reyes said, "Unfortunately, there is nothing on Earth that can change something back to normal."

Joshua went back to King Marco and said with regret, "I've tried everything but there is nothing I can do to get back to normal."

The king was laughing and said, "April Fools!"

Max, the Hypnotizer

by SOPHIA RAMOS

Max (his real name) was 21 years old and lived in a haunted house on a lonely street. A lot of people would go to his home because they thought nobody lived there. He was born in New York City and slept in a cave underneath his haunted house. Max was a scary-looking dog; his legs were crooked and his paws were not the same size.

Max could hypnotize people and could turn *into* anyone he had hypnotized. This was his secret. He did this by trapping any humans who enter his haunted house with a big net. Afterwards, he would go to someone else's house and ring their doorbell, hypnotizing whoever answered the door so that he could take their shape. He would repeat these same steps over and over because it was a cycle, which only lasted about three weeks.

It takes a lot of work to become a human; bunches of weeks and days to complete the process. Max didn't like to hypnotize kids because kids are so playful and love to play with dogs so much. The sound that Max made when he was upset was the sound of a *Rrrrraw!* and then he would throw his paws up and run around in circles.

Max's greatest fear was losing his powers, but his dream was to eventually become a person for real. He had a habit of barking until somebody paid attention to him and he loved kids because they played with him. He hated adults because they would get irritated when he barked. Max's most powerful emotions were triggered when he was disappointed, but he would often relax by lying on his back and drinking milk.

One day—a terrifying, scary day—a really ugly dog named Jacob came to his lonely street and went into Max's house without permission. Max was not there—he was still out in the world hypnotizing people. Max went quickly to his house and he saw the door open. When he got in there, he went upstairs and saw Ugly Junior with Jacob. They started to argue and fight, so Max tried to hypnotize him, but Ugly Junior also had powerful magic. Max kept trying to hypnotize Ugly Junior, but it didn't work. Defeated, he went outside to get some air.

He left to seek shelter in his underground cave. He wanted to regain his full powers so he could fight with Ugly Junior. He got full powers through a unique piece of jewelry he wore around his neck, which shot lasers. Confident again, he returned to the scene and saw that Ugly Junior had left.

When Ugly Junior came back, he wore special armor. Max saw that he had powers of his own. They started fighting, but Max knew this wasn't right.

"Stop, just stop," Max said, "I am sorry that we have been enemies all this time."

Ugly Junior and Max went back into Max's haunted house, where Jacob had also appeared. "What are you doing here?" Max asked, "I don't want to fight and I don't care what you say, you hear?"

Max walked away from Jacob. Jacob thought, *What in the world is he doing? I guess I will just go home.* Jacob left and Max was relieved because fighting him meant he was a bad person, which he did not want to become.

Max stayed home to relax and enjoy the fact that he did not want to fight. He went outside in the breeze for a little while. A cluster of people surrounded him so he started to feel puny. He became so weak that he was no longer as strong as a lightning bolt. He became very hungry and he still wanted to hypnotize, but he wanted to become a good person. His hunger grew stronger and stronger. He kept getting smaller, so he continued to go out and hypnotize in unsuspecting houses and as he did, he regained his strength. When this happened, nobody took care of him. He had to take care of himself for two weeks.

I am such a weak monster, Max thought to himself. *I have to hunt. I am already hungry.*

I go out every two weeks, leaving my gorgeous mansion like a bright diamond. I get lost in the city and feel so scared.

"I am going far, far away," he told his friend who was a human. "Far away."

He wanted to go home. He wanted to be remembered.

The Spirit of Janet

by NATALIE GUZMAN

nce there was a little girl named Janet who had long, black hair and eyes that shimmered like the beautiful ocean. She was 12 years old and had a love for dance. She was always bullied for not being the best dancer. They would tease her and say critical words like "ugly," "phony," and "fraud." She always dreamed of going on Broadway and dancing her heart out. Unfortunately, she got ill and passed away, and was never able to accomplish her dream of dancing.

In the year of 1960 (25 years after Janet passed), she rose from her grave and saw many new things about her town, Vuda. She saw some girls who had an amazing resemblance to the girls who bullied her. She was a red, raging bull ready to charge. She used her powers (which were the elements of the earth, like fire, water, and anything to do with nature) to make the little girls run away terrified and pee in their pants.

After another century passed and everything that she saw was different, like phones and high tech gear. She wanted to look around and see the differences in her town of Vuda. On her way downtown, out of the corner of her eye, she saw a dance studio called Cotton Candy Dance Studio. It looked like a big rainbow-colored sparkly ballroom and smelled like millions of roses. The girls in the studio were practicing a dance routine. She got ticked off as she saw a little kid throwing a tantrum over something they did not get, so she decided to cause some problems.

As she went into the studio, she saw a couple of little girls, but the people who really had her interest were the best girls: Daisy, Jordan, Emma, Star, and Maya. These girls danced as gracefully as beautiful swans swimming in a pond. Janet possessed Maya and started to make a lot of trouble. Janet started to make Maya push the other girls and say hateful words like "ugly," "phony," and "fraud." Those words kind of sounded familiar.

One thing Janet did not notice was that there were cameras watching her every step and move. The girls wanted to find out why their friend was doing this, so they went into their secret hideout in the dance studio and started to think.

"When did Maya start to act like this?" asked Jordan.

"When we were practicing our new dance routine," explained Star.

"Wait, I felt a weird, spooky wind pass by me when we were practicing our routine!" shrieked Daisy.

"Like a ghost? Yeah, right," laughed Emma.

"Could it be?" gasped Star.

"Maybe," muttered Jordan. Emma stopped laughing.

"I got it!" called out Daisy. She led them to the camera room.

They were very scared at what they saw, but they knew what they had to do. They went online to a website called www.monsters.com. They found out that you could strap the monster to a table, then use a vacuum to take out the spirit. Next, you needed to take a bottle and put the spirit inside the bottle, then throw or bury the bottle far, far away . . .

"That is all we need to do. Wow, pretty easy," said Jordan.

"I know, right?" agreed Emma.

"Let's go," said Star.

The girls were in such a rush to find a way to cure their friend that they forgot to finish reading the website. It stated that you needed to secure the bottle with a special liquid that could only be found in the deep end of the forest of the Haunted Hallows, inside a cave that was guarded by ugly monsters with sharp teeth and huge horns.

Meanwhile, the girls were thinking of a plan to strap Maya to the table so they could take out Janet's spirit. Jordan came up with the idea to lock her up in the room and put a projection over the table of a girl dancing to lure Maya. Once that happened, the girls would pop into the room like popcorn; some would hold Maya and the others would strap her down.

Everything went as planned. Maya was tied to the table, the girls had the vacuum, and now all that was left to do was to take out the spirit. As soon as Star turned on the vacuum, lightning filled the room, wind blew all around, and all you could hear was the horrible shriek of Janet's yell for help and her curse: "I will find you!"

"Is it over?" asked Emma when the lightning and wind went away.

"Only one way to find out," said Daisy.

Jordan, who was holding the bottle, held it up so everyone could see. They saw a dark, black, foggy wind, which they knew was Janet's spirit. The girls made sure Maya was okay (she was) and told her what happened. The look on her face was as if she had just seen an evil monster—times 10 (which she had).

The girls went to the ocean to throw the bottle away for good and make sure Janet was never seen or heard from again. Once they threw the bottle away, they cheered and went to go finish that dance routine.

•

A generation had passed. Some little girls were playing on the beach in the sand. They found the same exact bottle—opened!

ILLUSTRATOR: KYRSTIN RODRIGUEZ / STUDENT: NATALIE GUZMAN, PAGE 78

The One that Got Away

by STEPHANY ELIZALDE

nce, there was a wife and husband, and the wife was expecting to give birth to two eggs. They waited for their babies to hatch out. "I can't wait for my babies to come out!" exclaimed Mom. She was a new monster mom and felt excited.

When they came out, they were as happy as dancing trees because they were monsters. They named their two babies Michelle and Jayla. They lived on the bottom of the ocean. They had a little hole so nobody would steal from inside their house.

The ocean world was as dark as a city with no lights and was as cold as ice. They had seaweed as plants and pictures hung up on the wall. When they wanted to go to the surface, they transformed into humans.

"I have an idea. Let's go for a walk in the woods," Dad said, excited. They went to pick apples. The woods were full of green plants and you could hear crickets singing. But suddenly, some scientist came out of nowhere and trapped Dad by shooting a net at him.

"Oh no, my husband!" said Mom. Mom was as scared as if a ghost came out of nowhere. She was on land and jumped back in the water. In her home she kept her babies safe, but they would always ask where their dad was.

"Mom, where is Dad?" said Michelle. Mom tried to make them realize, but it was hard for her to say something that was not true.

One day, Mom came out of the house.

"I think it is a beautiful day to take a walk in the woods," said Mom. She was trying to look for her husband, but she couldn't find him. Unexpectedly, she heard screaming.

"Help me, please. Somebody help me!" screamed Dad.

She went to find out, and there was her husband. The scientist put him in a cage and put a lock on the cage so he wouldn't escape. His wife heard screaming and tried to find somewhere to hide so that the scientist would not spot her and trap her, also. She came up with a plan to rescue him. She sneaked in and then her husband spotted her.

"I will free you, don't worry," whispered Mom. She tried to free him, but the lock was too hard. She grabbed a hammer and smashed it open.

"Come on, let's go!" exclaimed Mom. Both of them escaped back to the ocean and into their house. They were all happy to see each other again. The babies were also happy to see each other and meet Dad.

"I'm so happy to see everyone!" exclaimed Dad.

After this, they never separated again. The scientist came to find them to apologize and tell them that he would keep their secret—that they were the last creatures of their kind.

The Thing that Came from Above

by JOSHUA PARSIO

larim lived on the southern part of the planet Glarth. Planet Glarth was lush, humid, and had lots of lakes that were as deep as oceans and as green as toxic slime. All of the monsters were gross, ugly, slimy, and horrible. They had sharp teeth and they were tall as redwoods, strong as bulldozers, and scary. They had five arms, but it was hard to tell because of all of the slime on them. They were as fat as elephants and each had 12 eyes and seven legs.

Dlarim was a good monster—not ugly, gross, or big because he cleaned himself up. That made the other monsters think he was weird. He had fewer limbs and weighed less than the other monsters, because he was smaller. That made him scared of the other monsters. He really wanted a friend that he could trust, but he couldn't trust anyone—if he told the other monsters that he was good, and who knows what they might have done? They might have put him into a special school to make him have a blank attitude. Then, he would not have been good *or* evil, helpful *or* unhelpful. He would not have had any feelings. Or, they might have brainwashed him to make him actually evil, and Dlarim did not want any of those things to happen.

Dlarim was working on making a spaceship to get to another planet to find a friend, but he couldn't tell anyone, because they would have gotten suspicious.

"I can't wait 'til I'm done building this spaceship!" Dlarim excitedly whispered to himself.

Dlarim was almost done with the spaceship. It was big enough for only one living thing and its luggage to fit. It had large holes at the bottom for the fire to come out so it could fly. It had one window on the only door on the spaceship. *VRRRR, BANG, BANG, VRRRR.* He drilled in the last screw. Dlarim turned all the switches on.

"Lift off in 10 . . . 9 . . . 8 . . . 7 . . . 6 . . . 5 . . . 4 . . . 3 . . . 2 . . . 1. Goodbye, planet Glarth!"

Dlarim laughed as the engines of the spaceship turned on, fire came out of its bottom, and it flew to who knows what planet.

The next thing he knew, he landed on a planet: Earth.

"Where am I?" Dlarim asked.

When someone saw him, she called the police. Two scientists named Sky and Jeremy were both very smart and had lab coats. Sky had curly short black hair and a below average height and weight. Jeremy had slick brown hair and an average height and weight. They'd found out about an alien on Earth.

"We have to get that monster!" Sky exclaimed.

"But how?" Jeremy asked.

"We have to find him and chase him down. We don't know how fast he can run or how smart he is," Sky answered. They had no idea. Dlarim had six legs and was as smart as Albert Einstein. The scientists tried to capture Dlarim and they chased him into my house.

When I saw him I was scared. I didn't know what to do.

"What are you?" I gasped.

"I am Dlarim. I am from planet Glarth. Can I hide here?" he asked. "The scientists are trying to get me."

"Yes," I said. "For how long?"

"As long as it takes for the scientists to give up," Dlarim answered.

"OK, but stay hidden from my mom. She will freak out if she sees you," I warned him.

On the third night that he was there, the scientists kidnapped Dlarim and put him in a car. They almost made it to the lab when Dlarim used his laser eyes to escape. He started running home.

The scientists learned from their mistakes, so they made a cage out of metal that couldn't be melted by any heat from Earth.

Dlarim's laser eyes were out of this world, literally, so he escaped again.

The rover on Mars soon found a type of metal that could hold Dlarim.

So, when Dlarim and I were playing at the park, the scientists snuck up behind him and captured him. He tried to escape, but the metal successfully held him.

The scientists were about to give him shots when I came in and tried to help him escape. I tried to steal the key from Jeremy, but he kept it in his pocket and he put a lock on this pocket. I tried to break the metal cage, but that obviously didn't work if Dlarim could not escape. When I went out of the lab, a UFO came, along with another alien like Dlarim!

I went to go talk to him and he was a good alien like Dlarim of the same species from planet Glarth. His name was Hsoj. I found out that he was from the northern part of planet Glarth. That part was cold and gloomy, and it rained every day. Hsoj came to Earth because he thought he was the only good monster, too. Hsoj and I made a plan to help Dlarim escape. He wanted to help because he was a good alien, too, and he thought it wasn't right for someone to lock an alien up to do tests. He distracted the scientists by running past them and having them chase him while I stole the key and helped Dlarim escape.

Three years passed as the scientists chased them down, but finally they gave up. After that, Dlarim and Hsoj came out of hiding and we all were friends. We went to school together and everybody heard about what happened. We played games. Not video games though, because with eight fingers on each hand, Dlarim and Hsoj would always win. We just did normal things that kids do, except that they are aliens.

Everything that happened after that was normal. Not really, because there was an alien living in my house . . . but you know what I mean.

Pluto and the Cursed Amulet

by ABIGAIL AGUILERA

luto, a 12-year-old monster with three legs and a furry pink-and-turquoise body, lived in Paris in a penthouse with a mall inside of it. She had super-speed—she was as fast as a fly—and she always wanted to travel around the world. Some places she wanted to go were Italy, Hawaii, Chicago, Arizona, New York, and many others. She took a yoga class every Saturday with her best friends.

She had a great view of the city. "You can see some of the most beautiful monuments from here," she whispered to herself. She was terrified of clowns, thunder, and the dark. And her job was to help people with problems around the world.

One day, Pluto got a call from a familiar and scared voice saying, "I need help!" Pluto thought it might be her evil sister, so she super-sped to get to her, but her sister didn't really need help. Her evil sister's name was Kelly.

It was common for Kelly to cast evil spells on her friends, taking their powers and making them disappear.

Kelly said, "I have something for you."

Pluto replied, "What is it? I don't trust you, Kelly."

"But I just want to do something nice for you."

"OK, fine, let's see what it is."

"Here, it's an amulet for you."

Pluto said, "Thank you!" She put it on her neck.

Kelly gulped, "It's beautiful!"

"Well, bye, Kelly. Thank you again."

"You're welcome." When Pluto left, Kelly hissed, "This is all part of my plan to take her powers away."

Pluto was wondering why her powers were acting up. They wouldn't let her do anything. She knew it must be the amulet. She was powerless for years. She tried everything she could to get the amulet off, but she couldn't. It was stuck!

"It's so hard not being able to have powers," Pluto cried. "I'm so not used to it. Now I have to learn how to drive because I can't use superspeed anymore."

Pluto was upset at her sister for years. Pluto was as quiet as a mouse. One day she was walking in the park and she saw her evil sister. She ran into her, so she talked to her, but she didn't really want to see her. Kelly felt guilty because Pluto was her sister and she missed her, so she removed the amulet and took the curse off of her.

Kelly sobbed, "I'm tired of being evil. I have no friends. Can we start over?"

Pluto wanted to forgive her because she felt sorry for her and believed she was probably lonely.

"Try your powers out," said Kelly.

"WOW! They work! Thank you so much!" Pluto cried out.

They became as close as salt and pepper.

Here We Go, Boo University!

by MARITZA MORENO

mily is a nice, kind monster. She's intelligent and peaceful, too, always helping homeless monsters. When she walks outside and sees a homeless monster asking for money, she'll give him $20 so he can get something to eat. Emily can fly and run faster than a meteor. She talks just like a normal 20-year-old girl. Emily loves to run to school, the supermarket, and the laundromat.

Emily was born in Chicago, Illinois. She just moved to Maxlandia again, where there is a university called Boo University. At Boo University you can learn what it takes to be an animal doctor. When you enter the main entrance, it's like an office. When you leave you have to sign out, and when you enter you have to sign in. You get to live in that big university. Emily sleeps in a hotel on campus.

Emily was sitting on the kitchen table eating a bowl of Mini Wheats. As soon as she was done, she went and got her suitcase and told her mom, "Goodbye. I am leaving for college."

Emily's mom shouted, "You got toothpaste, underwear, tank tops?"

Emily, annoyed, screamed, "Mom, I have everything! OK, bye."

Emily kissed her mom on the cheek.

When Emily was putting her suitcase in the car, her best friend came out. Her name was Natalie. "Hey, friend. Leaving for college I see," Natalie laughed.

Emily smiled. "Yes, I will miss you, Natalie. Maybe one day we will go to your college."

Emily hugged Natalie. Then she went in the car. She put the keys in the ignition, looked back at Natalie, and told her, "I know you will miss me, but you will see me in six months. Wait. If the university lasts four years, you will see me every six months."

Natalie said, "OK. See you in six months." Emily left.

Later, she exclaimed, "I am here finally. OK, I am going to start working. I wonder if I will make friends, or maybe I will not. I've got to think positive."

Emily thought she wouldn't make friends because she thought the other people might not like what she liked. "I know by the time I enter, I have to go to lunch, so I will sit and start to present myself."

By the time Emily entered the lunchroom, she would be able to get to part B. Part A was walking to the university and practicing what to say. "Hi, my name is Emily. What's your name?"

A girl who was sitting at that table told Emily, "Hey you, girl with the ponytail. Me and my three friends are sitting here, so back off."

Emily said, "Oh, sorry, I did not mean to bother you. I just want to make friends."

"Well, go eat under the counter next to the trash." In the trash, there were dirty bananas, burgers, and milk cartons. Emily sat there crying while everyone was laughing at her.

Two months later, Emily was thinking about how she would be able to see her mom and her best friend Natalie in just four months. Then, suddenly, Ana shut Emily's locker and said, "Hey, Emily, you got me and my friends in trouble. Now I need payback."

Emily said, "No, please. I did not mean to. To be honest, you guys got yourselves in trouble by making me eat in the trash."

Ana said, annoyed, "Whatever, now we can't get our phones and we have detention for two weeks. So thanks a lot, jerk."

Three months later, life moved on.

If I could just hold my tears of sadness inside, Emily thought. She was alone, but as soon as she turned around, Ana and her friends grabbed Emily and pushed her into a chair and mumbled, "I will put this helmet on to take control of your brain."

Ana wanted to take control of Emily's brain to keep her from telling a teacher about the secret room. When Ana found this secret room, she went to the bathroom and found the brain control machine. Emily put the helmet on her head and suddenly Emily took control of Ana's mind using her superpower.

Since Emily had a superpower, she could take control of anything that she did not like. Emily made Ana call security. Then the guards took the helmet off Ana and she said, "I will get you, Emily."

Emily replied, "I don't think so, friend."

After they took Ana, Emily teleported to her room and grabbed her suitcase, teleported to her car, and sped away!

The Homework Monster

by ANDRES RODRIGUEZ

here once lived a monster named Homework and he was 1,000 years old. He was so big, with 1,000 questions that were harder than a boulder to answer. He fed on students' knowledge and students who didn't know the answers. He desired answers. He bathed in knowledge. He slept in the book bags of children. It was scary and dark in there with lots of stuff like clipboards, pencil cases, books, and notebooks. He hated grown-ups and moms but loved teachers. He hated video games and loves students. He loved math and reading and hated getting dirty. This horrible Homework Monster had big claws that looked old.

Homework was born by the hands of a teacher named Al. Al wasn't always evil. He first gave homework to teach his students important things, but they never did their homework because they thought it was pointless. Al got crazy mad and started assigning so much homework. If students didn't do their homework, they would get a punishment—writing their name over and over again on five pieces of paper. He worked with the Homework Monster to make his students do their homework.

Al's dad was evil, and Al looked and acted like his dad. One day, when Al went home to visit his dad at his house in the suburbs, Al sat with his dad in the living and told him, "I'm going to be just like you." He didn't want to be evil like his dad, but he felt like it was already too late. His dad was a scientist who has a lab coat and messed up hair. He had glasses and every time you saw him, thunder noises appeared. When he was growing up, Al was always afraid of his dad.

I am unfortunately one of Al's students and I am in fifth grade, studying math. When Al gave me my homework, I went straight home to start. The whole way to my house, Homework was sleeping in my book bag. How did I know? The snoring gave it away. I was embarrassed because people could hear the sound and might make fun of me.

When I got home, I opened up my book bag. It jumped out and screamed, "Answer me!"

I was scared. I didn't know what to do so I just did what it told me, but it was so hard because it was math. Finally, I finished and started playing video games.

While I was playing, Homework got angry and yelled out, "Turn that off right now."

I told him, "No."

It got extremely mad at me, turning pink like a pig. It started destroying my house by throwing shoes around so I stopped playing video games.

When my mom came home, she asked me, "Did you do your homework?"

I told her, "Yes."

She checked it and told me, "This is not right."

Then, Homework got mad again and started destroying a whole bunch of new stuff in my living room—a TV, a vase, a bike, and a couch. He was a big, giant white paper flying around with the force of a strong wind. When he calmed down, I went to sleep. That's when he calmed down, too.

The next day I went straight to school with my homework because that homework drove me crazy. I turned it in to Al and he started to grade it. I screamed out, "I hate homework!"

When I got home, my mom screamed at me, "Who broke the vase, TV, and couch?"

I told her, "My homework did it," and she screamed more.

"How can your homework break stuff?"

I replied, "Um . . . "

She yelled out, "Best excuse ever!"

I told her, "Mom, I don't want to start a fight so I'm leaving to my room!"

She told me, "No! You made a big mess so you pick it up right now!"

"OK," I told her. "I don't wanna start a fight, Mom. That's why you won, Mom, but I will have revenge! Muhahahahaha!"

Oh no, I'm turning evil! Well, that's a good thing, I thought.

Fifty years later, Al passed away but his students were still alive, healthy and strong. Now they have children. They were very happy living with their families until their children went to school. All of the parents started crying non-stop.

Their children asked, "Why are you crying, Mom and Dad?"

They told them, "You don't want to know why, son."

The son asked, "Why not?"

Mom told him, "Because . . . you don't want to feel the pain we had when we were children . . . "

The Homework Monster—you could never escape him.

My Monster Kid

by WILFREDO RAZO

M y monster, Kid, was born on both Halloween and Friday the 13th at midnight. Those nights were stormy and rainy. Kid is seven years old and his parents raised him until he was one. Then his parents were kidnapped by humans. His master, Creepy Crawl, gave him his name because Kid is smaller than his friends.

Kid is a shapeshifter who can shape shift into anything he sees. He has started monster training with Creepy Crawl, but he is afraid of his master. Kid lives in an attic with slime and dead bodies. The attic is cold and dark. The smell is toxic. He sleeps in a grim reaper bed. Kid's house is full of the scary stuff he likes.

Kid loves to play with his toys—they are zombies, demons, ghosts, and more. He watches scary movies like *Scary Nights*, *Friday the 13th*, *Halloween*, *Haunted Christmas*, *Haunted Campout*, and *Haunted Tales*. He does not tie his shoelaces. He has super senses and loves to sniff and play with his food. He yawns in his sleep all the time. He walks straight with his arms tired. He runs to smart kids and scares them. His eyes glow like crickets.

Kid is bad at handling kids. He is always very angry when his friends forget his birthday. The sight of spiders and crickets scares him a lot. He hates humans but loves to eat pizza for lunch because it is his favorite food. He does not like kids who cry because the noise annoys him so much.

Kid has one friend and his name is Charlie. Charlie thinks he is smarter than everyone and annoys Kid a lot. Charlie goes to Kid's attic for a sleepover. Kid sleeps without his blanket because he gave it to Charlie, who ripped it. Charlie loves it ripped because he loves to rip stuff. Kid can't afford a new blanket and doesn't like sleeping with the ripped one.

Kid has a twin brother named Stinky who died a long time ago. He is buried in a cemetery. Kid dreams of having another brother who is bad and loves to scare kids, too.

Kid always reads before going to bed and he writes in his diary every night.

I LOVE
TO RIP
STUFF!

Warrior Kittens

by SILVA FLORES

nce there were three kittens: PB, TL, and Stormcloud. PB was a tan kitten with white on her neck and on her stomach. She was a domestic shorthair. TL was a black kitten that also had white on her stomach and neck. Stormcloud was a gray and white kitten with white on his paws, face, neck, and stomach. They were all 12 years old. They mainly lived in the forest or woods with many trees and foliage. PB was born in a human's house. TL was born in a bush. Stormcloud was born in a warrior's den. They could sleep anywhere cozy.

PB was intelligent, swift, and patient. TL was bright, dark, and sweet. Stormcloud was tough, very swift, and enthusiastic. They could all morph into anything. They could meow and speak in English. They could also kind of speak Dog. They could turn into cheetahs with wings and go faster that way.

PB's secret was that she was a kitty-pet by blood but a clan kitten-cat at heart. Her fear was rats and would always get Stormcloud to kill the rats. Her dream was to be in normal form, but with Pegasus wings. TL's secret was that she was an orphan kitten, but she found a new family with Stormcloud and PB. Her fear was losing her friends. Her dream was to be a chef. Stormcloud's secret was that he wanted to be a warrior. His fear was killer birds. His dream was to eat a footlong Italian sub with chips—when he peeked outside the forest, he saw an ad about it.

Sometimes they left their claws out after killing prey or attacking. PB loved to see new things. Stormcloud loved attacking things. TL loved hunting. PB hated Two-Legs (humans). Stormcloud hated spiky leaves because when he got stung by them, TL, PB, or the medicine

ILLUSTRATOR: MEGAN PELTO / STUDENT: JOSHUA PARSIO, PAGE 85

cat had to heal him. TL hated getting dirty after cleaning herself. For PB, when someone hurt her neck it made her mad. For TL, when someone reminded her of her parents, it also made her mad. For Stormcloud, when someone teased him about a killer bird being around he got mad—really mad.

They all felt relaxed when they slept, napped, or daydreamed. PB felt kind of intimidated was when she was near cars. TL felt intimidated when other cats hissed loudly at her. Stormcloud felt intimidated when foxes howled. He was not afraid of foxes, he was just afraid of their howling.

These three kittens lived in the woods, near a little pond. TL was the swift one; she ran like the wind. PB was the smart one, planning attacks. Stormcloud was the athletic one. He *loved* challenges.

They didn't just live near those peaceful things. They also lived near a noisy street with restaurants, malls, and their nightmare: the animal shelter. The animal shelter was their nightmare because they were clan-born or they were rogues (stray cats) that joined a clan. They heard that humans would just take a cat and *keep* it. The humans were monsters to them. They heard that cats were the property of the human who adopted them. None of them had ever gone into the shelter but people would try to get them.

Besides the animal shelter and the loud noises during the day, they'd had a good life. The worst thing was the other clans. The other clans attacked, but not often. When they did, it was bad. They would get the strongest warriors. The strongest were very burly—their clan almost always won. These three kittens had special powers—to shapeshift into anything— anything at all.

When they played with each other they raced, jumped on one another, wrestled, play fought, and played with the bottle lids that they found. They could play with some bugs but they were too slow, although they would play with butterflies and moths.

"What do you want to do today?" asked Stormcloud, bored as if there was never anything to do.

"Want to hunt?" PB asked.

"Sure," TL said excitedly, "but where?"

"The lake!" PB exclaimed.

"All right," said Stormcloud, satisfied. "Let's go."

They came home with fish in their mouths but when they walked to their dens, the emergency alarm was going off. They put their fish in the food bucket as fast as they could to get to the center of their clan.

"What's wrong?" PB exclaimed.

"Are we out of food again?" a random cat asked.

"No, we sent out our three best spy cats: Bluefur, Firetail, and Sunray. They came back with important news," Violetstar announced.

"We have found out that the Blue Clan has planned to battle us again and will try to make us join the clan if we are defeated," Firetail said.

"They will come in a month. We will prepare by getting the Yellow Clan to join us, but if that does not work, everyone will be training. The old cats will train to help the medicine cat, Shortear," Sunday announced.

"The Blue Clan is strong, but we can be stronger!" Bluefur yelled encouragingly.

"Go to your dens, eat, and then go to sleep. The first thing at sunrise, we will train. Our master warriors will go to the Yellow Clan, " Violetstar announced.

They went into their soft leaf-and-moss bedding and fell fast asleep. The wake-up alarm was urgent. The cats had breakfast mice. The master warriors traveled to the Yellow Clan to ask if they would join their clan. The old cats went to train with the medicine cat. Half the warriors went to hunt for food to eat later on, and the kittens went to training with two warriors.

The first step was pouncing—they learned to pounce directly on their target. Next was slashing at the bark on the trees. The last training was wrestling. They wrestled some fake mouse toys that they stole from people that crossed by with a "PetSmart" bag (whatever that was).

After 29 more days of a lot of different training, they were really prepared, but the Yellow

Clan didn't want to join. All the old cats were trained to help the cats that would possibly get injured or sick.

The battle was here. They were ready.

"Meerrooww!!!!" The battle had begun!

TL jumped on another cat, Stormcloud wrestled another cat to the ground, and PB hissed at another cat. This battle lasted two days and two nights. The three kittens battled on the first day and the last night. They, thankfully, won.

"What a battle!" Violetstar cheered.

"The battle between our clan, the Red Clan and the Blue Clan was hard, but we have won. No cat died but there were a few injured cats. They are with the medicine cats now. Most cats weren't injured very badly and they are all right. They just need some medicine on the scratches to keep out infection," Shortear said.

"Yay!" cheered the whole clan.

They raced back to the den, which was a large stump with a hole in the top and a large hole on the side for a door. In front of the "door" hung soft moss. The three kittens ran inside, going toward their soft moss bed, fell over, and in one second they were sound asleep.

THE END!

"Hey, this is the end?" PB asked. "No it's not."

"Good!" Stormcloud yelled.

"Will this conversation continue?" TL asked.

"Nope," PB said.

"OK," smiled Stormcloud.

TL yawned, "Good. Can I go back to sleep now?"

"THE END *FUR* REAL THIS TIME!" they all screamed at the same time.

The Cherry Hair...?

by ALEXANDER RODRIGUEZ

One day, Gobatroll was at his cave with checkered floors and a big TV, and he was getting wet from something. Gobatroll had the body of a centaur, the face of a troll, and a nose with bushes of hair.

He said, "Hey, stop wetting me!" but every time he turned around, nothing was there, and so he went to go dye his slimy hair at his favorite salon. When he got home, he got wet again.

He said, "My red-cherry hair, gone! Because of this water!"

His son Damien woke up and screamed, "Dad! Why do you keep yelling?"

Damien is skinny with four legs and slimy hair. His favorite sport is basketball and his favorite color is purple. Or red. Or green.

Gobatroll said, "Because this water that is coming out of nowhere keeps getting me mad! Mad as a baby that woke up!"

His son asked, "But why?"

"I just got my slime dyed. It got wet and washed right off!"

His son asked, "Do we have anything to drink?"

Gobatroll said, "The only thing we have to drink is water, but good luck finding it. I can't even find out how I'm getting wet!"

His son said, "Dad, wake up!"

He asked, "What do you mean, son?"

His son said, "You are in a dream."

His son pinched him, and he woke up. When Gobatroll woke up, his son was drinking water. Gobatroll jumped, and it spilled on him a little. He said, "Where is that coming from?"

His son said, "You squirmed and spit water on yourself like 100 times."

Gobatroll said, "Oh well, how convenient."

His son said, "Literally."

So then Gobatroll said, "We need to get rid of this water that keeps spilling on me!"

His son said, "But Dad, how? It's not like there is a sign in our cave that says *Catch me*— the water comes out of nowhere. And besides, I had a bunch of water but you kept squirming and jumping and you made me spill it every time."

Gobatroll said, "Oh yeah . . . "

His son said, "But there is one thing that we can do."

Gobatroll asked, "What is that?"

His son said, "Dye our slime!"

Gobatroll said, "Now, now, listen. We cannot do that without amazing, cool, glow-in-the-dark dye!" So they went to the salon that had fish tanks and music playing and posters of fake detailed cars all around. Gobatroll was getting his slime dyed when all of a sudden he heard his son screaming, "Oh my god, this is amazing that I am getting my hair dyed!"

Then Gobatroll's stylist said, "Dad?" and the Gobatroll said, "Jack?"

Jack had the body of Gobatroll with black hair with a red mohawk. They hugged. On the day Damien was born, Jack ran away just to explore but forgot his way back and Gobatroll never found him.

Jack said, "Can I go see Damien?"

Gobatroll said, "He is your brother, go right ahead."

Jack went to see Damien, and Damien said, "Jack!"

Jack said, "Hey! I missed you guys!"

Gobatroll said, "Guess what?"

Jack said, "What?"

Gobatroll said, "You wanna come home?"

Jack said, "Yes!"

Later that night they went home and Gobatroll said, "Wow, it's late." But Jack and Damien were already sleeping on the ride home. Gobatroll said, "Oh brother, I am talking to myself and the souls of the walls. Wow, Damien fell asleep as quick as getting a flu shot."

Later that night Gobatroll went upstairs to watch TV in my room when I remembered that Jack and Damien were still downstairs sleeping! he said, "Oh well, my favorite TV show is on."

And Gobatroll never got wet again.

The Big Jelly Old Monster

by ORLANDO SANTOS

elly Old Monster's mom always called him Blobby. He looked like a 20-foot-tall green jelly and you could see through him. When he sat or fell on you, you went inside him. He was like jello, and when you eat jello and put a spoon in it, you can see the spoon in there. This Jelly Old Monster came from a failed experiment. His mom also got created in the lab. They escaped from the lab and now the Jelly Old Monster robs food from people because when he was small, all of his family lived in the streets. They asked for money and kids started to say bad things to him because he was not a normal person. He also devoured the food that he stole. He hated people because when he was small they made fun of him. That's why the Jelly Old Monster stole their food.

He was also scared of cats. When he was five years old, he loved cats. He caught a cat and, while he was trying to carry him, the cat scratched him. He went to the first store to steal food but it did not have food because it was Cool Games. There were only video games. He got so mad he shook and splattered green goop everywhere and left the store. Everywhere he walked, he turned everything green like bright limes. Then he went to a second store and the owner caught the Jelly Old Monster stealing food. The Jelly Old Monster was stealing food because he did not have money or food.

The owner of the store yelled to the Jelly Old Monster, "What are you doing to my store?" He kicked him out of the store.

Then he went to a third store called Fresh Food found what he was looking for. He did not get caught by the owner of the store as he snuck around to find 40 bags of all the foods he liked. Little by little he took the bags out of the store. The bags overflowed with pizzas and chicken wings. He took the stuff to the garbage can where he lives. The garbage can smelled really bad but he devoured the food. He got very full and he left the other 34 bags behind, so when he was starving he could go back.

The Jelly Old Monster got money by robbing a bank and asking for some money on the street. He wanted to have enough money to buy a house, but the stolen money wasn't enough. He also got more money by getting a job constructing buildings. He started constructing little buildings for little kids and selling them. Then he found a house for sale with food in it. He bought the house and he felt extremely happy because he didn't have to smell rotting stuff anymore.

After one year passed, he ran out of money but the old owner of the house started to pay so the Jelly Old Monster could still live in the house. He stayed and the owner still bought him food. The old owner decided to pay the rent because the Jelly Old Monster told the old owner that he did not have money. The old owner was 57 years old. He lived next door to his old house and felt alone so he wanted a friend. They started talking the first day they met each other.

Now they take turns sleeping in each other's houses because they live by themselves and they don't want to feel like they felt in the past by themselves. They pass all the holidays together and celebrate the day they met each other.

The Dead Universe: Curse of the Arisen Knowledge Keeper, Universe One

by JAIYA OVID

ere I am, standing in the mountains, thinking about my past. Thinking about all that my family has been through. Thinking about all the secrets my family has kept from me and the future that awaits. As I watch the sun come up I think, *How did I get here? How will I tell him what I saw?* I realize that I have other duties besides just sitting around in my favorite spot, staring at the mountains and daydreaming about my true relatives.

As I shove my binoculars, map, and water bottle in my backpack, I hear his footsteps, but they are not coming toward me. I hear his familiar footsteps snap on a nearby tree, and the sound of his handmade leather boots inside our home, the oak tree. I hear him in his special place, the library. I wonder what the ancient book is saying to our young wisdom keeper.

I wonder what has happened. Something's wrong—he does this when he's deeply confused. I always want to comfort him. I always have this urge because he is my brother, and we depend on each other and take care of each other. But I know that when he's in this state he could get deeply frustrated, so I don't bother him.

He always seems calmer when he's reading. He feels like the library is home because my family are the knowledge keepers. We keep society in balance because everybody has a task, and anyone who does not do their part is banished.

This has helped us all survive, but in so many years I've never felt such great jealousy— the pure evil monster who tears out my heart out each day, eating my compassion. I ask myself, *How can I feel this way toward my own brother?*

He saved my life when wolves came to our village four years ago, when we were six years old. I was playing in the wonderful, magical meadow, which is full of flowers and peacefully grazing deer and smells strongly of lavender. This magical meadow was my favorite spot, but when ferocious beasts lurked in the grass as I roamed, I feared becoming prey. While I was picking flowers and eating wild berries, I saw the most beautiful wolf ever imagined. It stared at me with dark gray eyes, irises like the crescent moon and fur like winter, with grayish-black markings around its eyes.

I did not think it would attack me because I could see the wisdom though its eyes. It did not appear menacing, but when I turned and walked toward the woods it attacked me. I was left, bleeding and alone. When my beloved brother came back from a hunting trip and saw what the wolves had done to the village, he went out of his way to help keep me alive.

A couple of months ago, our leader said that we needed to recruit and train more soldiers because an enemy leader wanted to have a war.

At least . . . I heard a messenger from the government say that. There are many things I long to know.

Once, the elders saw two army messengers coming and hid us in the attic. When I asked why we hid, I got no answer—just, "Some things are too complicated for a vulnerable child to understand."

This upsets me, when I am not told anything.

After our leaders said they needed more soldiers, adults started acting extra strange. More and more messengers came, delivering more army demands. My family doesn't talk about this at the dinner table anymore. They keep things from me now.

Our friend Simon's dad disappeared the night after he refused to go with the army.

"I saw the army," Simon said in a shaky voice.

"Tell me everything," I snapped. I sounded angry, but most people had given up. I haven't.

Simon went looking for his dad and never returned. They sent search parties to look for him. I volunteered for search duty, but they wouldn't take me.

"We won't take people who are not of our kind," the leader of the group said. "Plus, you're only 11 years old."

"This work is for adults," one of the 22-year-olds added, just to be rude. I decided to look for Simon myself. I searched as far as I could go, but I never found him. A messenger gave us the news that Simon was dead, but I didn't believe it.

Today, I listen to my brother as sincerely as ever. The news he is about to deliver could make this the best moment in my life. He may have found Simon.

I am so overjoyed that I blurt out, "You found him! Where is he?"

When I realize this is only a possibility, I feel a mixture of embarrassment and anger.

"Calm down," my brother said. "But I saw a clue that Simon might be nearby."

I can't believe it. The government claimed that Simon was dead. Puzzled and confused, I try to believe this impossible news, but remember how I was taught that the government is loyal to its people.

I did not think it could be so cruel and hateful because that would only mean one thing—they made Simon go back to the military. Realizing this, I drown in despair. There would be no saving him now. But my instincts tell me that there is a way. Finally, it comes to me—an idea that could change the nation.

After being hit with a tsunami of emotions and spinning in a tornado of ideas, I calm down. I must investigate the royal family and government of the past—the origin of our villages.

There was once a place called Earth, and there were people called humans. We are descendants of them. There was a rumor of a city, a place like no other with buildings like giants. Only one person lived to tell the tale of the past—the wisdom keeper.

I wonder if Mom will approve of me spending the night in the magical world of books, even though I have to help her build a new shelter along the oak tree path. I promised to help with the secret building method that protects it from the storms, a secret passed down from generation to generation. I start heading back to the village, but change my mind.

Instead, I head toward the wisdom keeper.

The Lonely Boy

by BEYRALI SANTIAGO

The year was 1947: I was in a destroyed bed with the spring sticking out. I thought to myself while I was in my abandoned house, *Hmmmm, nobody has ever talked to me. Maybe no one ever talks to me because of all the secrets that I have. Or maybe, because nobody knows my name is Jack. I got into this house because of all my secrets, like how I can time travel and run really fast. Or maybe, nobody talks to me because of the hunger I have every five seconds. Or maybe, because of the way I look when I look at the things I like to eat. Or maybe, since I have a human body and werewolf hands, the tongue of a cow, and the fangs of a vampire.*

I time-traveled back to 1947 because I thought people would be nicer to me. But even in 1947, people would look at me and run away. Once, I asked a grumpy lady (who had a tremendously beautiful wart), "Are you in line for that cashier?"

She hissed, "What do you think?" and turned her back on me. At that moment, I realized I forgot to buy the apples.

When I go to stores, people look at me and run away. I feel lonely and empty. The only reason I go into public spaces is because I just want a friend. I don't care that people run away because I know that I will make a friend soon.

I time-traveled to a street in Magic Cahook in 1845, because that's where I have a lot of good memories. I wanted to see the little house where my parents used to live. I looked to my left and saw a little boy sitting and crying, with his knees to his face and his hands tied around his legs.

I went up to him because I heard him say, "I'm lonely!"

He talked to me for a little while, saying that he trusts strangers more than his own bloodline and needed someone to talk to. But then, he saw my face.

"I have to go!" he gurgled.

I time-traveled to my abandoned house in 1947 again. I was all alone and thought to myself, *I need to go back to the street called Roseland.*

On my way, I saw another little boy crying and sobbing, "I want a friend." The little boy saw me and said, "You again."

I looked again and realized—it was the same little boy! I thought, *How is this possible? This is the same little boy I saw earlier?*

The little boy tempted, "Now, you can be my friend." I tried to make a run for it, but he was already right by me.

I finally asked, all confused, "Are you OK?"

The little boy gulped, "Yes, I am lonely."

"I know that feeling," I responded as I looked at the floor. "Why are you crying, boy?"

"Because everyone in my family died and I am in an orphanage."

"Do you want me to take you out of here?"

"Yes, yes. Please take me out of here!" the little boy cheered.

"Hang on!" I shouted as I grabbed the little boy and teleported.

The little boy and I kept going to different places all over the world. We soon reached the final destination. As soon as he opened his eyes, the little boy shrieked, "Where are we?"

"Welcome to Puerto Rico!"

The little boy asked, "Why here?"

I replied, "Because it is very fun here with beaches, fun, and anything else you could want." The little boy felt safe and comfortable with me, his new buddy.

"My name is Henry . . . I am immortal," the little boy said.

"Hello, Henry. I am Jack. I have a human body and werewolf hands. I have the tongue of a cow and the fangs of a vampire. I'm immortal, too."

The Monster Who Wants a Girlfriend

by ANGELIZ RODRIGUEZ

losereto is an 826-year-old monster who lives in his childhood closet. It's a dark place packed with a lot of clothes and shoes.

Closereto is mean, ugly, and determined on the inside and out. He is creepy with scales that change colors, and spikes. He has the power to change into any kind of shoe or clothes. He likes to put his hands on his chin like he's thinking. He gets around using other peoples' bodies.

Closereto fears going to the laundromat. He dreams to be the ruler of all closets. His secret is that he never takes baths and doesn't have a family. He likes drawing, making stuff out of clothes, and riding his bike in the closet. He loathes the meanest of all closet monsters, CLOS. CLOS triggers his emotions.

When Closereto is not thinking about CLOS, he likes to relax on the beach, or in the winter he stays inside his closet and drinks hot cocoa and watches TV.

When Closereto was born, he was scaly and green. Also, he had skin as rough as a rock, with pointy teeth and a long tail with spikes. The years passed and he learned how to transform into clothes or shoes. The way he transforms is by thinking really hard that he is going to transform. He had his own closet to live in, but he was as lonely as a homeless person. He thought there was something missing and he wanted girlfriend.

He tried to look for a girl monster but he couldn't find one anywhere. He went to every store in the world but he couldn't find a girlfriend. He was so sad he wanted to disappear. CLOS, who is hostile, always teased him because he didn't have a girlfriend. "Aww, little Closereto has no one to be with, so DEAL WITH IT," CLOS yelled. That made Closereto feel awful.

I HAVE AN IDEA, LET'S GO BOWLING

CLOS was tall, black, and hairy. CLOS and Closereto were enemies because on Black Friday CLOS and Closereto both wanted a flat-screen TV. They went running to the electronics section but there was only one left. They had a battle and Closereto won, which made CLOS really mad and hate Closereto even more. CLOS knew that one day he was going to have revenge.

One day, Closereto went to a very fancy restaurant with everything made out of glass. The glass was as bright as a diamond. He spotted a girl monster sitting all by herself. Her name was Closereta. She was pink all over and always wore a bow on her hair. He went over to her and started talking to her. "Hello, nice to meet you," Closereto said.

They became really good friends because Closereto paid for her food. Then one day they met up at a coffee place. They started talking about their lives and what they do. "What do you do for fun?" Closereta asked.

"I like to go bowling," Closereto replied.

"Hey, I have an idea, let's go bowling," Closereta suggested.

"Great idea, let's go," Closereto replied.

They went bowling and had a great time. But a few weeks later, they got into a really big conflict because he left her hanging in the movie theatre and she got mad. They stopped talking and being friends. The days passed and they did not even talk for a minute.

Then, one day, Closereto bumped into her at the store! They did not say a word to each other, they were just in shock. Then Closereto broke the ice: "Hey, how are you doing?" he asked.

"Good, and you?"

"Good," replied Closereta. Then she walked away from him.

Just then, CLOS came by the store and teased Closereto, "Aw, did you lose your friend? Or should I say, GIRLFRIEND?"

Closereta heard what CLOS had said to Closereto and got super mad, because she had just come back to say "I'm sorry" to Closereto. She started crying and ran away. Closereto saw her, but he just walked away.

Then, CLOS thought of an idea to kidnap Closereta. He wanted to kidnap her to get revenge on Closereto from the day Closereto won the TV. CLOS broke into Closereta's house and took her.

Closereto heard about the kidnapping on TV. He got so furious and he knew it had to be CLOS. He tried to look for her and he found her! He found her in a cabin far away, because Closereto knew CLOS's secret cabin. He conquered CLOS by having a wrestling fight. Of course, Closereto won. Then, he called the cops and the ambulance.

After that, Closereta wasn't mad at him anymore. She knew she may have overreacted about the teasing from CLOS. Closereto and Closereta were done with CLOS's teasing, and they walked away.

ILLUSTRATOR: THOMAS QUINN / STUDENT: JAIYA OVID, PAGE 109

Who's There?

by RUBY ECHEANDIA

essica Williams was a five-year-old girl with beautiful brunette hair and hazel eyes. She was playing with her blue and red blocks on her living room table.

"Wow, I made a castle, Mommy, look!" Jessica squealed in delight.

Her mother, Kate Williams, was in the living room watching Jessica while she was on Face-agram and shopping online for coffee.

"How nice, sweetie," Kate replied. Kate thought she kept Jessica indoors too much, so she told Jessica to go play outside. Jessica wobbled outside, leaving her blocks on the wooden floor.

Jessica had only been playing outside for about three minutes before she screamed. "Mommy, I found something and it's kinda freakin' me out!"

Kate rushed outside and asked, "What? No one is here."

"But Mommy, she is in the bushes!" Kate looked in the bushes and stood in horror as the creature rose up from the bush.

"A-duh!" whispered Jessica, trying to act like a teen.

Kate screamed, "What is that?"

There in the bushes stood a red-eyed demon with fangs like a vampire and beady eyes like a snake—a human-like creature, looking calmly back at Kate.

It said, "Give her to me and don't even think of calling the cops, or else."

"Never!" Kate cried, pulling Jessica inside and calling the police.

It seemed as if the police were never going to come and investigate, but soon everyone could hear sirens. As the sirens grew louder, Jessica hugged her mom even tighter. The police searched the backyard, from the flower pots in the garden to the cement on the street. They searched every crack in every stone and every piece of dirt in the ground. Kate offered to help.

The policeman huffed at this. "No ma'am, we are the pros. We don't need help, so leave us to it."

When they were finished searching, the policeman packed up and said that he had not found anything.

"It was here," Kate pleaded.

"Not now, it left," said the policeman.

"I'll give a call if I see it again," Kate responded.

"Please don't," said the policeman under his breath.

"Hey!"

"Time to go boys, this witchcraft makes me feel eerie, and anyway, monsters are so fake. I've heard of having a childish mind, and this will be reported if you don't stop."

"It's real!"

The men walked out, ignoring Kate.

"Mommy, why are all my clothes in a backpack?" Jessica asked her mom as she packed everything up.

"We are leaving this place," her mom said.

"Why, Mommy?"

"The monster is going to take you," her mom responded and shivered. "Why is it suddenly cold?"

Kate slowly turned around, and there it was: the creature staring right at her with those beady eyes. She swooped in as fast as an eagle and raced off with Jessica.

"Mom!" Jessica yelled as loud as her voice could go.

"No! Please, no!" Kate screamed with tears in her eyes.

Cara the monster took Jessica to a dark cave, lit only by a small candle and fed Jessica a juicy, red, seedless watermelon. Jessica wanted to refuse, but she was starving. She ate the watermelon cautiously.

"Why do you want me?" asked Jessica.

"Because I've always wanted someone to love. I saw you and thought you were perfect for me," Cara replied.

"I want my mommy!" cried Jessica.

"Sssshhhhhh, I'm your mommy now," shushed Cara.

Cara knew that her own family would find her, eventually. Her father was known to pop up anywhere and everywhere. Suddenly, they heard a man's voice that Cara recognized.

"No, not now," Cara whispered as she put her hands over Jessica.

"Cara, I know you're here! Come out so we can talk, now!" yelled the voice.

"Never!" Cara screamed as she held onto Jessica.

"Who's that?" Jessica asked.

"Shhh. If you don't come out, I'm coming in!" The man stepped in with a dirty suit and old, messy, white hair. He looked like he'd been searching everywhere in the world for Cara. He looked at Cara, then looked at Jessica. "Why do you do this?" asked the man.

"Dad, it's time I stay like this."

"And keep a child hostage?"

In stepped Cara's mother, holding Jenna's hand. Jenna was Cara's six-year-old sister.

"Stop yelling, dear," said Cara's mother.

"Mommy, I'm scared. What is that thing?" asked Jenna, pointing at Cara.

"It's Cara," said the dad.

"No, Cara is nice and pretty, and that is . . . not."

Cara stood there and looked as though she had just realized what she had turned into. She fell to the ground.

"What have I become? A monster is what I am. No more!" A flash of light came out of thin air and she emerged as a human.

"Whoa, that really was Cara," Jenna said with surprise.

Cara squeezed Jenna and then hugged her parents.

Kate walked in, pretending she hadn't just hitched a ride with Cara's parents. They had found her while she was just walking on the side of the road, crying. Cara's parents asked why she was crying. Kate said that her child was kidnapped. Cara's parents looked at each other knowingly and took Kate immediately to Cara.

"I believe I should take Jessica and leave," Kate said.

"Wait! Kate, wait!" Cara pleaded.

"Yes?"

"I'm sorry, I just turned around and realized I wanted a daughter. Maybe not a daughter, but someone to love. And now I know who that is," Cara said a bit too sappily. "It's my family."

"Why don't we go to my house for dinner?" Kate suggested. They all drove to Kate's house and ate chicken with mashed potatoes and corn.

"Thank you so much," said Cara's mom.

"Can I go play with Jenna in my room, Mommy?" Jessica asked politely.

"Yes, dear," Kate responded. Jessica and Jenna raced as fast as horses to Jessica's room while Cara's parents watched *Ms. Bri Bri Gots More Talent Than You!*

"What is this?" screamed Cara's mom at the top of her lungs, enjoying the show.

"Now you're the one screaming," said Cara's dad. "This show is the best!"

"Sorry, but yeah, it's really good," Cara's mom agreed.

Cara and Kate were talking about life and politics. "Politics are very—I don't know, I don't find them interesting like adults do," said Cara.

"That's true, I don't get them either," said Kate as she flipped her hair sarcastically. "I think like a teenager, but I'm trapped inside the body of an adult."

"Umm . . . Kate?" Cara asked sheepishly.

"Yeah?"

"Can you help me with my homework? Like, I love reading and the class, just not the homework."

"Sure," and they ran to Kate's room to do the homework. At the end, Kate and Cara became friends, Jessica and Jenna became friends, and Cara's parents had found their favorite show, *Ms. Bri Bri Gots More Talent Than You!*

The Night of the Shadow People

by ESTEBAN FLORES

nce there was a kid named Henry, a nine-year-old blond-haired boy who wore a red and black striped shirt. He loved horror films such as *Jaws* and *Friday the 13th*, *Dracula*, and *Nightmare on Elm Street*. He liked those movies so much that when he grew up, he wanted to make his own films that were so scary they would make you jump out of your skin.

Meanwhile, in a dark alleyway, four shadows were whooshing around, laughing and giggling. Their names were Calvin, Tiny Tim, Tony, and Fred. Over 50 of these shadows lived in a dark spot under the sewers. One of them had a white star on his chest. His name was the General of the Shadows and he was the First Shadow. He had an assistant called Ned. Ned was the Second Shadow.

One day, while Henry was at school, the little shadows entered his room and slept in the shadow of his bed. When he got back, he heard something say, "Ouch!"

He leapt off the bed and saw all four of the shadows coming out of the bed. Henry didn't know if he should speak or keep quiet. He said, "Hi," and they said, "Who are you?" all at the same time. "We're the Shadow Kids," they said in unison.

Henry asked them tons of questions like "What are you?" and "Where did you come from?"

Then, his mom called, "Dinner time!"

"Uh oh!" Henry said, rushing downstairs and pretending nothing had just happened.

He sat down at the table. He was having chicken and broccoli.

After dinner, he returned to his room.

"Where are they?" he wondered to himself.

"Boo!"

"Eeeeek!"

The Shadow Kids laughed, "Ha, ha, ha, heh, heh!"

"Henry?" said his mom.

"Hide!" Henry whispered to the Shadow Kids. They hid in his coats' shadows.

"Are you OK?" his mom asked while standing at his doorway.

"Yes," replied Henry.

"Are you sure about that?"

"Mm-hmm."

"Positive?"

"Yep," said Henry confidently.

"OK. Would you like to go to the store with me?"

"Yeah!" Henry said. He had a weak spot for shopping. He grabbed his coat that Tiny Tim was in and he left.

At the store, Henry bought peas, milk, chicken, some Franks Red Hot, Cholula, Churros, Chrisso, mild taco flavoring, minced turkey meat, and some wheat and white bread.

He got home and told the shadow kids, "OK, no more distractions. I'm taking you all back home. Now, where do you live?"

They all pointed to the street. Henry only saw the manhole cover that was extremely rusty.

"You live down there?" he asked. They nodded.

"Aw, snap!" They went down the manhole cover.

"OK, here you go!" Henry said, "See 'ya!"

"Wait," said the Shadow Kids.

Dang it, he thought. "What is it?" he asked.

"You have to take us!" they said. On the way, they ran into five Shadow Guards.

"Halt!" said the Shadow Guards, who were guarding the vault that the shadows lived in.

"What do you want?" said Guard One.

"I want to return some kids who are bothering me," said Henry.

"NO HUMANS!" the Shadow Guards screamed.

Henry and the Shadow Kids ran as fast as they could. The laughter of the guards got louder. "Ha, ha, ha, ha, ha, HA HA HA HA HA."

Henry and the Shadow Kids forgot where the manhole cover was until they saw a ladder.

"Perfect!" said Henry.

He went up first until—*Whip!* Henry went down until he hit the ground. Henry, the Shadow Kids, and the guards had a big battle, like boxers in a 10-round fight. Henry and his friends won, and Henry ran home to put on black makeup so he'd look just like a Shadow Kid. After the battle, they couldn't get back into the shadow vault—not even the Shadow Kids. As Henry was taking off his makeup, he saw a dark flash go right past him. Then two more, then five more. He rushed outside to see millions—probably trillions— of shadows.

Henry ran to the town square, where everybody was screaming and running for their lives as the shadows whooshed around. Just then, Henry realized what the shadows were made of.

"These shadows are part human, and part fear," he said. "We have to stop encouraging them!" Henry got on top of a car and shouted at the top of his lungs, "STOOOOOPPP!"

Everyone froze and looked at Henry. "You have to stop acting like they are scary," he said. Nobody moved.

"What?" said Fred.

"We have to stop encouraging them!"

"Ohhh," said Fred.

"What do you mean?" asked Tiny Tim.

"The shadows get stronger when we show fear because it's what they are made of."

"Let's get going," said Henry. None of the townspeople moved. The shadows tried to spook them, but they wouldn't budge. All of a sudden, *WHOOOSH!* The fear and shadows came off of all the Shadow People, and they were only human.

The Shadow General turned out to be the General of the United States.

The General had become a Shadow Person when a bomb nearly detonated on him during a war long ago. The bomb ended up being a dud, but fear escaped the bomb and entered the General in a big, dark flash, immediately turning him into a Shadow General. This fear spread all over the world, turning others into Shadow People.

"Henry," said the General. "Our nation supports you."

"We support you, too, General," said Henry.

"So, to celebrate . . . "

"Uh."

"We will . . . "

"Umm."

"We're having a party!" shouted the General.

Terrazeni's Revenge

by FERNANDO PEREZ

ong ago, there were two young men named Sky and Jack who had special powers, one with fire and one with ice. They were nice people with a great sense of humor. They came from Egypt and they were extraordinary people who saved lives, even when there was a chance of dying while doing it.

During their lifetime, there was also an insanely powerful monster called Terrazeni. He was known as the Emperor of the Universe. He was the cruelest and most careless creature. He didn't have a heart of love, he had a heart of evil. He was as mean as Dracula and a devil mixed together. He mind-controlled people. He also absorbed people because he always felt like a freak and was jealous of normal peoples' lives. He had dimensional strength and the power of destruction. He was green with spikes on his body and all over his arms. His feet had long toenails that were sharp as swords. He had teeth like a vampire, and red eyes that cried spicy tears. He was abandoned in the ocean and lived inside a rock.

One fine day, Sky, the man with fire powers, and Jack, the man with ice powers, were farming. They sensed something moving in the wind. It was Terrazeni. He attacked Sky and Jack's village because he wanted to mind-control the women there and possess Sky and Jack's dual powers. In the village there lived younger men like Cole, who had the power of nature, and Turner, who had the power of speed. All together, they tried to protect the kids and women in the village, but they were not really sure if they could do that because Terrazeni was as powerful as an alien that could touch the Earth with his finger and destroy the whole galaxy. Terrazeni arrived on his tornado, and it was fast like a cheetah, or faster. It was a dangerous tornado with spitting spikes.

Terrazini said, "Give me your elemental powers or die," but Sky, Jack, Cole, and Turner denied him and started to battle Terrazeni. Terrazeni with his wind power blew them all away. Then, he destroyed the village and attempted to mind-control some villagers, but the women protected their kids. He thought he could make them do anything just by screaming at them. He could make birds and planes in the sky crash into each other. He could make people sleep in the middle of driving a spaceship. But in this village, he was finding it hard to control anyone.

That's because there were four kids, Fernando, Alexis, Orlando, and Alex, who each had the powers of their fathers. Sky, the father of Fernando, gave his son fire. Jack, father of Alexis, gave his son ice. Cole, the father of Orlando, gave his son the power of nature. Alex was the son of Turner, who gave his son speed.

The mothers ran with the sons far away from the village, but Terrazeni's rays of mind control hit the moms as they ran. It only took 14 seconds for their minds to be fully controlled by Terrazeni.

"Run!" yelled the kids' moms. Their names were Liz and Janet, Gaby and Koko. Fernando and Alexis didn't want to separate. Orlando and Alex took Fernando and Alexis far away from the village. Fernando, Alexis, Orlando, and Alex went to the city to be protected from Terrazeni.

The city was as beautiful as a fresh waterfall in the forest. Sky, Jack, Cole, and Turner rose up with bloody bodies, then Sky sourced fire from his hands and threw it to Terrazeni. Terrazeni blocked it, and with his power of destruction he summoned skeletons, some spiders, wind people, and killer robots—a whole army.

Turner, Cole, Jack, and Sky got ready to battle. They channeled their powers and started battling but there was no point of fighting—Terrazeni kept summoning more and more. Cole did this technique called "blinded." He hacked the power of nature and used a sun technique. Out of his eyes came light—white light, really bright—then the light started hurting their eyes, so they closed them and when they opened them again they were gone. The monsters went to find them.

Terrazeni really wanted to absorb them. Terrazeni went back to the ocean and stayed there to nap—he slept lazily in this ocean known as the Ocean of Evil all day. The monsters went looking for Sky, Cole, Turner, and Jack. Sky and his friends hid in a cave, but the monsters didn't stop looking. They could feel them, close. The spider put a web on the whole village, but the cave was close enough to the village that they got out of the cave, fast. There, the monsters spotted them.

The skeleton quickly raised up his bow and shot Turner in the leg and he was injured. Sky went back to help Turner because Sky was an optimistic person but they shot him, too, and Jack and Cole got spider-poisoned. The monsters took Sky, Cole, Jack, and Turner to Terrazeni. Terrazeni was happy and the monsters were proud.

Terrazeni said, "You don't have to fight, you're trapped already. Do we want to do this the easy way or the hard way?"

The easy way was to let yourself get absorbed, the hard way was to get attacked by 1,000,000,000,000 monsters and get tortured, which Terrazeni loved to do.

Then Sky said, "The hard way."

Cole said, "You're kidding, right?" Cole didn't want to battle 1,000,000,000,000 monsters. Then Terrazeni reversed his summons of the 1,000,000,000,000 monsters, because he wanted to fight the kids himself.

Sky quickly charged all his powers. His body turned into fire and the Earth shook. Turner, Jack, and Cole did the same and together they made a power ball. They all threw their power at Terrazeni and he flew away, but the blast of their combined magic was so powerful that it created another dimension to trap Terrazeni. Terrazeni sent an egg flying into the dimension. Inside that egg was a baby monster: Terrazeni, Jr.

Orlando and Alex were hurt and tired.

Orlando said, "Leave me and Alex here," but Fernando and Alexis decided they must stay together. Orlando and Alex went home to rest while Alexis and Fernando trained. The skeletons saw Orlando and Alex and one with his savage bow shot Orlando. Orlando went down.

Alex got worried. "Orlando! Wake up! Are you OK? What happened?" But they shot him, too. Alex screamed.

Fernando and Alex turned around. "Did you hear that?" Fernando said.

"Yes," Alexis said. Fernando and Alexis went flying.

"Speed up, Alexis! Don't stay back, catch up," said Fernando.

"Wait, I don't wanna waste energy. We might need it," said Alexis. They went to the village to see what happened, and Alex and Orlando were not there. Fernando and Alexis were worried. They kept looking.

Fernando screamed, "A skeleton!"

Alexis roared, "Make him talk!"

Then the skeleton cried, "Fine, just don't hurt me. They're in the cave from the north, it's 20 miles away," he said.

They were shocked and quickly went to that cave, but it was far away. Meanwhile, Alex and Orlando were trapped in the cave with spiders.

"Stop this! Let us out!" said Alex and Orlando. They were scared. The skeleton bent down on his knees and Terrazeni, Jr. came out.

Terrazeni, Jr. was a baby—one year old—and every two minutes he turned one year older. Also, his powers got greater as his age went up.

When Fernando and Alexis arrived, they said, "This cave is a maze."

"Wow, we're never gonna get out," moaned Fernando.

They separated and heard baby laughs. They found Terrazeni, Jr., and made a lot of noise. They prepared to fight and they were scared.

Fernando and Alexis saw Orlando and Alex trapped, and they wanted to save them by finding extra help. Trying to save them alone was too dangerous. They decide to make a blast so powerful it blew a hole in the cave.

"Run! We're gonna die!" said Alexis.

"No," said Fernando with a tired face. They defeated him.

"We defeated Terrazeni," said Alexis. They were super happy. They looked for Alex and Orlando. But suddenly, Terrazeni, Jr. grabbed Alexis.

"Give me Alexis or I will shoot my strongest blast," said Fernando. "I don't care if I waste all my powers on you!"

Terrazeni said, "Go ahead. You will not just get me, you will get your friend!" Fernando felt hopeless.

Terrazeni said, "Don't move or I will ruin him." Fernando didn't move, but Terrazeni was hurting him.

Fernando lamented, "This is all my fault, I should have never let Orlando and Alexis go to the house." Terrazeni was about to absorb Fernando, but Fernando got out and saved Alexis. An arrow shot Fernando and he fainted, but Orlando got up and hit Terrazeni from the back. Alexis heard all this and woke up. Alex got Fernando up and his big sister Adriana came to help them with her power of fire as well.

Fernando woke up very slowly—he was hurt. Alexis was happy that Fernando woke up and he started crying of happiness. They all were there now for the battle. Terrazeni couldn't handle the power of Fernando and Alexis. They were all exhausted. Terrazeni disappeared and they never saw a monster like him ever again.

Max and Rex

by AILANY ARROYO

ax, a 16-year-old monster, was walking to the big river to drink water and find berries and meat to eat. The big river was lined with rocks and scattered with deer, fish, and butterflies, too. His long fur was black and white and his eyes were as red as hot lava. Max lived in a tunnel near the big, raging river. Max liked to tell jokes and acted crazy silly. He screamed and ran around in circles. His friends would laugh and tell him he was amazing. He *was* amazing. Max had superspeed, running in circles as fast as a supersonic airplane. When he was happy, he clucked like a chicken.

Max's best friend was a wolf-monster named Rex. They were best friends all of their lives and were raised in the same foggy forest near the river. Max and Rex liked to play hide-and-go-seek together. They went apple picking and swimming together in the river on most days. Max's favorite thing to do was juggle apples. Even though they were the best of friends, Max and Rex argued a lot. Rex had a bad temper and got upset when his friends took his things.

One day at the river, Max saw his friend Rex in the distance and it looked like he was bullying a bear. Max decided to walk over to Rex and the bear.

Max said, "Stop! Leave him alone!"

Rex explained, "This bear took my shoe."

"No I didn't," replied the bear.

"Stop lying to me! I saw you near my tunnel earlier."

Max said, "Maybe this is all a misunderstanding. I borrowed your shoe without telling you. I'm sorry."

Rex apologized to the bear and gave him a high five. The bear asked, "Do you think we can be friends now?"

Everyone felt overjoyed and, of course, Rex responded, "That would be super cool!"

One foggy night in the forest near the river by Max's tunnel, Max wandered by the apple trees and big rocks. The night was creepy but he loved his home.

Max remembered the time he fought with Rex because he had said, "Rex, your shoes look ugly," and Rex was sad.

"That's not nice," Rex said, before remarking, "Well, your hat looks ugly!"

Max was really mad and shouted, "Well, your shoes are pink!" They started fighting. They stopped fighting and Max said, "Sorry," and Rex apologized, too.

Max was crazy good at juggling apples and Rex wished he could juggle apples and asked for help. Max showed him how to juggle apples and Rex was so happy. Rex juggled at night and did not sleep.

Max said, "Go to sleep!" but Rex refused. He could not stop juggling in the night even though he was really sleepy. Finally, he went to bed.

He woke up and saw that Max was eating and Rex wanted to eat, too. Max started walking to the river and was drinking water.

When he saw Rex, he yelled, "Rex, come here!"

Rex heard Max and he yelled back, "Max, where are you?"

"By the river!" he shouted. Rex ran and saw Max by the river, swimming. Rex ran into the water and they went home again together.

Rex wanted to stay outside and play in the rocks with sticks, and mud, too. Max asked him, "What are you doing, Rex?"

"I'm making a toy!" Rex said.

"That's so cool."

I'M CRAZY GOOD AT JUGGLING APPLES

"Thank you!"

Lucky the Fox invited Rex and Max over to her house later.

"I'm grilling outside," she said. Max and Rex agreed to come over and they went to her home. She said, "Welcome to my home!"

Max and Rex were so happy to discover Lucky the Fox had a pool.

"Do you love it?" Max asked.

"Yes, we do like it," Lucky said.

Rex said, "Let's play in the pool!"

They jumped into the pool, and soon after, it was time to eat.

ILLUSTRATOR: RICH SPARKS / STUDENT: ISABELLE GARCIA. PAGE 138

Snaky the Monster

by ALEXA CRUZ

ILLUSTRATOR: PHINEAS X. JONES / STUDENT: MARIE FLOWERS, PAGE 142

naky the monster lives in the zoo by himself. He has no family and he sleeps on the floor in a cage. He's black and brown and has a little tongue.

Snaky is angry because he wants to eat people and he can't. Snaky hides in the tree because he is scared the birds might try to eat him. He changes his color to orange to match the leaves.

Snaky is scared because he doesn't want to sleep in a cage anymore. Today, he went outside to the water to find food. He ate a fish.

Then, Snaky screamed because the people were touching him.

The Amazing Journeys
of Failure and Kiana

by ISABELLE GARCIA

t Brentano School there was a monster named Failure who lurked in the basement. Everyone thought that Failure was like a troll under a bridge. The kids would be absent the days they had an assembly. He loved when kids got F's, D's, and C's. This monster detested A's. He also did not like kids being mean to him. He looked like a big troll made up of the letters F, D, and C! He also looked like a normal person but much bigger. He was a big daredevil.

Brentano was first built a long time ago, when it was as shiny as a new glass sculpture. Every kid was afraid of the monster. Kiana, a super smart kid who was new to the school, was the only one who dared to go to the basement. She was not scared of Failure.

Kiana got all A's on tests. Failure did not like her at all! After a year, Kiana made lots of friends and tricked them to go down to the basement and see Failure. She tricked them by making them think they were going outside to play, then grabbing them and pushing them into the basement at the last second. Her friends were terrified.

Failure wanted to put a temporary spell on Kiana's friends, but would have to touch the person to do it correctly. Failure touched Kiana's arms and bellowed, "*Fail all tests by Failure! You are done for!*" Then, the Kiana and all the smart kids all got F's, D's, and C's. They got suspended five times.

Failure soon realized his magic was permanent, so he tried to find out Kiana's name which was necessary to undo the spell. Failure wanted to make it up to her, because no one liked him and he wanted to make lots of friends.

Failure tried to get up to the next floor but the security guards wouldn't let him in. Failure had to think of a plan, so he got a dictionary and used a long piece of string to tie it to the lower stairs, near the auditorium. He roared, "Up to the first floor!" as he threw the dictionary-on-a-string toward the security guards. The dictionary smacked each of them, and they fell down the stairs and rolled out the door. Failure ran up the stairs and shouted out the door, "I did it! I got to the next floor!"

Failure spotted Kiana and asked her to tell him her name. Kiana walked away and screamed, "Never! I will not give you my name."

Failure begged and begged. He stopped the spell so Kiana and her smart friends wouldn't get any more F's, D's, or C's. But the spell was not done yet. Failure could not undo the whole until they returned to where the spell was first cast—otherwise, it would be permanent! So they went to the basement.

Kiana screeched, "Let go of me, please!"

Failure worried, "I am helping you. This is for your own good!"

Failure undid the spell and Kiana said, "OK, thank you."

"You're welcome."

Kiana and Failure became best friends. Every day when Kiana went to school, Failure would grab a Lunchable and give it to Kiana because the school lunch was so bad. At recess, Failure would play with Kiana—hide-and-seek or freeze tag—and after school they would go to the movies or play a board game.

Failure and Kiana were the best of friends in the whole galaxy. They did everything together.

The Wolver's Adventure

by ETHAN ESTES

hen the world was born, so was The Wolver. He did like his mom and dad for a while but began to hate them, so he left to become a reaper. He was not a normal reaper, but a human with reaper-like powers. He could bring people to the underworld and was instantly good with a scythe. He became bad, and was like a volcano full of lava when he got angry.

The Wolver was a reaper of magic and skill. What does a reaper do, you ask? He rules the Reaper Palace. Other reapers are not as powerful because they don't have the Wolf Scythe, which has an empowering effect. The Wolver is good with a scythe but he is best with the Wolf Scythe. He does not do much with it, so it's like he's carrying a dead bee around. It's a secret. He quietly told us, "Don't tell anyone."

The Wolver rules his empire from the Reaper Palace with harmony and his secret is that he does not like to kill with his Wolf Scythe. He uses his magic not to kill, but to hypnotize, which is almost like dreaming. It's like a lucid dream about going to the Reaper Palace, but the people wake and find that it was no dream.

Don't tell anyone this, either. The Wolver's main fear is that his minions will discover that he is a wimp who does not hurt anyone. He also has a mild fear of bunnies, because bunnies bring happiness.

When a war began, The Reaper Palace started getting crowded and full of people, because when the people died, they all went there. Let me take it back a little bit to understand the past.

Before all of this, The Wolver was confused because he had magic but could not use it. He was as useless as a dead bee. The Reaper Palace remained empty for a very long time until "the right person" was ready. But that person was actually the *wrong person* and when The Wolver realized that, he started putting everyone to sleep trying to find the right person, but he never could.

He thought out loud, "Does this person exist?!"

He got angry and evil. Bad things started happening. Volcanoes erupted, earthquakes rumbled, and there were hurricanes, tornadoes, and tsunamis. Everything bad started coming and The Wolver was aggravated because he could not find the right person to fill the Reaper Palace.

Lightning raged and the volcano's lava became scorching, raining harsher with tsunamis more colossal than ever before. More and more people came to the Reaper Palace but no one was the right person. The reason The Wolver wanted the right person was because he was working with the world to keep it in peace.

But then, The Wolver finally found the right person! His name was Alex. All bad things stopped. Alex was not a bad guy and The Wolver liked him. They became friends.

Alex and The Wolver only fought once, over a mineral. A very rare mineral called Qutonium—a yellow crystal that glows and hums and is so rare that the last time it was found was when time started. It was not as useful back then, but now you can meld it with your mind to make it stronger.

A battle had started over the Qutonium. Alex had won in the battle in a kinda cool way, but really all he did was knock The Wolver out.

So then, Alex melded the Qutonium into great, flying, godly armor. He flew out with all of the Qutonium, but realized it was not *normal* Qutonium, but an altered version of it that the gods made!

Alex made it into really powerful armor so he could fly and save the world from destruction with his Holy Light. He went down in history with fame and glory.

And now, The Wolver can't even fight Alex, because Alex has the holy armor with automatic evil-vanquishing powers.

The world is safe now because of Alex.

Chesley's Life

by MARIE FLOWERS

irst, I have to take you back a long time to about six years ago, when Chesley was just a normal monkey exploring the forest. Now, he is a 56-year-old monster.

One day, out of nowhere, a monster called the Master appeared. It looked like a mini-person with a pointed nose and ears, and pimples on its face. Its clothes were made of leaves and it had boogers coming out of its nose. The Master started to chase Chesley around the forest, and Chesley ran away because he was scared. When the Master pulled the monkey's arm, some snot got on the monkey. The next thing you know, the monkey turned into a monster—a really weird one. Chesley became short, with ears that looked like pineapple slices. His nose and hands were pointed and his fingers were smooth and pointed, like someone had shaved the tips off of celery stalks. He had one green eye.

Chesley lived in a very dark forest where trees do not grow, inside a cave the Master had taken over. There was snow and bugs everywhere. In the cave, there were rooms for the crazy monsters, the sloppy monsters, and the scary monsters. All of the monsters were animals that had been turned into monsters.

The Master was the only creature on Earth who was born a monster. When he started to grow, he had powers, and snot coming out his nose. His snot went through the animals' fur and into their skin, like an infection. But instead of infecting the animals, it turned them into monsters.

Humans didn't know that these monsters existed, but they might destroy the monsters while they are out hunting. The Master threatened to release the monsters back into the forest if they didn't listen to him, but he really couldn't do anything. If the monsters got caught by humans, they could just tell them that the Master was making monsters.

One night, Chesley snuck out of the cave and met another monster, who told him that the Master's threats weren't actually true. Chesley started to disobey the Master's orders, and the Master threw him out of the kingdom, just like he had threatened. What the Master didn't know was what would happen when the other wild animals found Chesley.

Chesley told the animals of the forest about his past and the monkey he used to be, and that he just wanted to be a normal monkey again. They remembered him from before and believed him. They had been wondering where the missing animals went, trying to find out who had been taking them. They planned a war against the Master.

The queen of the forest, who was a peacock, was sleeping, so the animals woke her up. While she got ready to use her powers, her butlers talked to each other.

"What do you think would have happened if we hadn't told the queen?" Maria asked.

"There would be no more animals because, eventually, the Master would infect all of them," said Jonathan.

Jonathan's twin brother, Jason, started laughing. "That's not going to happen."

"Yes, it will," said Jonathan.

"No, it won't."

"Yes, it will."

"Hey, hey. You guys need to stop," said Maria. "Can't you see the queen is trying to work?"

"Stop!" screamed the queen. "I can't concentrate with you two yelling and fighting. I need to do this spell."

Chesley felt weird. He said, "Ow."

"Shut up," said the queen. "Don't you want to be how you were?"

The queen used her powers to turn Chesley back into a monkey!

Chesley took the animals to the Master's secret cave and all the animals came with their claws out. They went in and chased the monsters. In the middle of the attack, the Master said, "Hurry up, Chesley, we need to destroy these animals." But then, he turned around and saw that Chesley was a monkey again.

"Chesley? Is that you?"

"Yup," said Chesley.

During the fight, one of the cheetahs scratched a monster's pimple and infected green stuff oozed out fast. So much came out that it overflowed the cave. The animals tried to walk through it but it was like swimming instead.

When the Master came out and used his powers to shake the place, all the infected stuff slid out. The monsters were fine, but they had nowhere to live because the cave was gone.

After that, the monsters stayed away from the animals. If they went to war again, the same thing would happen but they wouldn't be saved—what the Master did could only happen once. That was how his powers worked.

The animals went home happy and safe, and the monsters did not bother them again. Chesley stayed a monkey, and because of what he did, he was made king.

The Life of the Six People

by BLANCA CHIMBO

Teddy was a monster who hung out at the ice cream shop that smelled like juice and soda. She loved to buy coffee ice cream and cold water. Coffee ice cream was Teddy's favorite ice cream. Teddy was kind, and fluffy as a cloud. Teddy had two buttons on her eyes. Her favorite color was purple and her most favorite food was Popeye's chicken.

Teddy had a soap that smelled like juice and soda, to remind her of the ice cream shop. Teddy's little corner where she slept was white. Teddy liked relaxing on the couch with my dog and with my cousin's dog, too, whose name was Max.

Teddy was active and loved to be outdoors. She would wait for me when I was at school and have a good conversation with me when I got home. She would ask me how my day was at school. We liked to talk about how our days were.

Teddy liked to help keep people safe. Teddy would rescue them from danger. Teddy had good friends. Her friends also helped save the world. Teddy liked when I was safe. Teddy liked to eat, and if a place was on fire, Teddy would help.

Teddy never wasted time. She knew what to do every day—she never wanted to lose time because she had a lot to do.

"Today was incredible!" Teddy would say. "How was your day at the park?"

"I had an amazing day," I began.

"Oh no," Teddy said. "There's a fire in that house. We have to check to see if there's anybody inside."

I said, "Good."

Teddy got the hose from next door and stopped the fire from ruining the building. The fire was so strong, it was breaking the building.

Teddy and Fluffy were talking about how to tell the people who lived in the house about the fire.

Fluffy decided, "I will go tell the people about the house."

Teddy said, "OK."

Fluffy said, "I am going to help them build a new house."

Teddy found the person. His name was Zeus. He was just a normal person with cool stuff. He said, "I don't want a new house. I could buy a better house."

Fluffy shouted, "Yes, if you have the money. But if you don't, you need to earn it!"

Zeus said, "OK, I *would* buy it but I don't have the money. I thought I had it, but I don't."

So Teddy and Fluffy helped Zeus by making him a makeshift house to use for a little bit until Teddy fixed his house. Zeus cried, "Thank you!"

Then Teddy left to buy stuff for Zeus. Zeus was so happy that he started singing a song.

When Teddy and Fluffy got tired, they went back home with Blanca and her dog. Fluffy, Teddy, Blanca, and her dog drank hot chocolate and lemonade. On the last day of school, Blanca brought Teddy and Fluffy to the party, and they met all of Blanca's friends.

They shouted, "Play with us!"

After that, the four of them drank lemonade and then drank some more.

Dr. Confuse: Adventures of Friends

by ALONDRA RUVALCABA

ne day, a very energetic baby named Dr. Confuse was born. Everyone thought he was mean and one day he would have to take anger management classes. He wore blue pants all the time. When he was a kid, he turned into a monster. He looked like an ugly human with a super long beard and a lot of fur. His family were also monsters who looked like horses. He lost a lot of friends when he became a monster. When he was 23, his family moved away to a far away country. He prayed for his family and tried to persuade them not to move, but he was too late.

Dr. Confuse had a total of 15 friends and wanted to be popular and for everyone to love him. He says I am his best friend. He loves to come to my house in the afternoon and help me do my homework, play, and watch TV with me.

He asks me, "How did you find all of these shows?"

I answer, "I just flipped to different channels and found this one."

He screams, "It is super fun!"

We watch *Liv and Maddie* and *Austin and Ally.* Dr. Confuse loves to wear t-shirts that are related to the shows.

Dr. Confuse gets sad and scared when it's windy and there is thunder. He calls me and screams because he is scared.

"Can I come over?" he asks.

"Sure," I say.

"Thank you."

Dr. Confuse lost his best friend, Sabrina, three years ago because she caught on fire in a terrible accident. He was so sad that he punched a garbage can. He gets so mad when anyone says her name. Once, someone said, "Sabrina," and Dr. Confuse punched a wall and it broke. He had $400,000, but after he punched the wall he had $200,000.

He asked me, "Do I still have a lot of money?"

I answered, "Yes, you do."

A bully named V was jealous of Dr. Confuse because he had an iPhone 8 Plus, and V only had an iPhone 5. They were going to fight about it. Dr. Confuse screamed, "I will get you, V!"

V screamed back, "Try!"

They both got grounded because of the fight. When they got out of their punishment, Amaris, a mutual friend, decided to pretend to be trapped in an I Heart Burgers. Dr. Confuse went to go rescue her, then V came and interrupted his rescue mission. They were both striving to save Amaris.

Dr. Confuse screamed, "You again! Well, I am going to save her first."

V screamed, "No, I will!"

They kept on fighting to save her, but Amaris explained that she was just pretending to be stuck. Dr. Confuse got mad and tried to punch Amaris. He did not really mean to, he just got mad and lost it. He gave apologies to Amaris and was so sad that he stopped trying to be a hero. Later, Amaris told Dr. Confuse that he should still save people because she believed in him.

One day, he saw flashing lights downtown and he went over to see who needed help. Duck Trump was stuck in the sewer, where it was dark and gloomy with a lot of trash.

Dr. Confuse went down into the sewer to save him. Right at that moment, V crashed into Dr. Confuse, which made him drop Duck Trump! V did not want Dr. Confuse to save Duck Trump because then Dr. Confuse would win the contest of who could save the most people. Dr. Confuse lost most of his followers on Insterbook after everyone saw him drop Duck Trump. He did not try to save anyone for one month.

Months later, Dr. Confuse was walking by a school. The school looked big, red, and colorful, and it was made of bricks. The playground was blue, big, and had slides, swings, and red monkey bars. He saw a kid stuck on a slide, screaming for help. Luckily, Dr. Confuse pushed the kid down the slide, and he was saved.

When he was watching TV at my house later, he saw that his save was in the news! Everyone watching the news ran to tell Dr. Confuse that they loved him.

He had accomplished what he wanted.

Ella and the Slimeball Monster

by FRIDA ROTHEIM

Hi, my name is Ella. I'm 12 years old. I have light brown hair and blue eyes. I'm usually alone at school or just sitting somewhere listening to music. I get all A's in school.

I have an annoying seven-year-old brother named Eric and a mom who always feels guilty. My mom has curly blonde hair and wears a business dress. My dad is always interested in and asking about everything. He has brown hair and wears a shirt and brown trousers.

One night when I was furious with my life, I saw a green, slimy monster come out of the closet. I shouted, "Mom! There's a slimy monster in my room!"

Mom was a little bit fearful and confused and asked, "It wasn't me who scared you . . . Right?"

I was not surprised that she thought *she* did it, so I piped up, "No, Mom! And you have to stop thinking that you've done something when you DIDN'T!"

I think that I said it too loud, since she almost jumped to the door from where she had been.

Eric came into my room and laughed, "Ella is a baby. Ella is a wimpy kid. Ha ha!" He was playing pirate, so he was wearing pirate clothes with black boots and a fake sword.

I became inflamed and shouted angrily, "Be quiet, Eric!"

Eric became terrified and cried, so he went to his room. My dad then came in and asked why I shouted at my brother.

"Dad, he said I was wimpy, and YOU punish ME? That is insane," I said.

"Yes, I'm sorry," Dad said. "I am going to punish him after I've asked you about something."

I was angry and deranged. "What do you mean?" I asked.

"He-he," he laughed as I gave him a weird look. "Anyway . . . Why did you shout about a monster?" he said.

"Yeah, about that. There was a monster in my closet who said, 'chchkkk, chchkkk,'" I explained. "It was so gross. Slime came out of his mouth!"

"But Ella, you know that there are no monsters in this house," Mom and Dad said. "You have to stop imagining things."

"I'm not imagining things." I said. "It is true that I saw that monster!"

"No honey, you just saw some clothes," Mom said.

I was angry. No one wanted to believe me, but I was right. When they left, the slimy monster came out of the closet again and slimed all over the floor. I didn't see the monster then because I was too angry to turn around, but I saw it when I was leaving to say sorry to Mom and Dad.

"Hi Ella, I'm Slimeball," the monster said. "I'm not dangerous. I need your help to capture a witch named Miss Evil."

"Why do you want to capture her?" I asked.

"I was once a human being," the monster said. "Miss Evil put a spell on me and changed me into a monster. I have to catch the witch and break the spell." He told me that we had to go to a monster shopping mall, where we could get a map to help us find the witch.

I wanted to help him, so I packed some things to bring with me.

When we finally got to the monster shopping mall, we found the monster maps store. We asked the clerk if he had a map to help us find the witch.

The clerk looked in a drawer and picked up a map. "This is the map you guys need," he said. We gave him two dollars for it, and then we went outside to go to the forest.

The forest was not far away. We walked for 30 minutes and got there before dark. The plan was to find the witch and make her break the spell to turn Slimeball back into a human. The man at the monster maps store told us that the witch was a mean lady and that we had to be very careful.

Slimeball and I looked around the forest the whole afternoon. When it got dark, we climbed a tree and found a small cabin in the branches where we could sleep.

We were just falling asleep when I heard a sound on the ground. I looked to see what it was and saw Miss Evil down on the ground. She didn't look like a witch from the fairy tales. She wore witch clothes and had neon green hair. She had a wand in her pocket, too. She looked really scary, and I became a little bit afraid. But I knew that we had to do something if we wanted to break Slimeball's spell.

I woke up Slimeball, who had fallen asleep. We climbed quietly down the tree and followed the witch. She did not notice. We followed her for a while before we could find a place to capture her. When she was in front of some rocks, I threw a lasso around her body. I pulled the lasso as hard as I could to tighten it. Then Slimeball and I tied Miss Evil to a tree. She was very angry.

"How can we break the spell?" I shouted.

"Only I can break the spell," Miss Evil said.

"Can you then break the spell for me?" I asked.

The witch took the magic wand and said, "*Bibbity, bobbity, boo, get dumb Slimeball to be himself.*"

After that, he was an old man again, like 78 years old or something. He had grey hair and wore an orange shirt and grey trousers. He had a little bit of slime on his clothes.

"I have to go home now because my mom and dad are going to be looking for me," I said. "I don't want them to call the police."

We untied Miss Evil from the tree, and then I went back home. "That was the best day ever," I said with a smile.

Mom and Dad had just been watching TV and thought that I was in my room. Eric had fallen asleep, so he was okay, too.

What I didn't know was that the witch was after me because I had tied her to that tree.

ILLUSTRATOR: CHRISTOPHER GIVENS / STUDENT: RUBY ECHEANDIA, PAGE 119

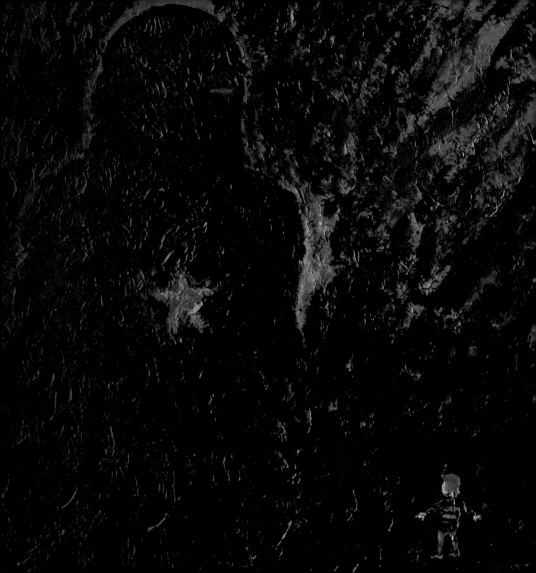

The Adventures of the Night Gorilla

by ALEX MOROCHO

long time ago, there was a monster called Jefferson who was born in Texas, Florida. His habitat was the forest and he lived after dinosaurs existed. He was half-gorilla and half-human, because he got infected by a gorilla who bit his neck. He had black-colored fur with white-colored stripes across his body. He was five feet tall and three feet wide, and he weighed 345 pounds. Jefferson lived in the forest with his friends and he was 20 years old. He slept in a tree alone with his blanket made of leaves. He had the power of strength and he even sounded like a gorilla—*ohh, ghrh, urgh*. He grunted "Gruh" to people that he didn't know, but they got along together.

He fought for his food with gorillas and hunted for his prey. He got along while his friend played a board game, and by talking and chatting with gorilla friends that he met. He relaxed in the lake in the hot water by the rocks. His secret fear was winds, because he got disturbed when his blanket of leaves blew off and he couldn't cover himself. The gorillas didn't know that Jefferson was half-human and half-gorilla, but one day they noticed that he had a superpower that was a sturdy force, so that whenever he got shot or touched, he didn't feel it.

When Jefferson slept, his powers shut off. Later, when he felt wind and branches touching him, he got scared and went to his guidebook. It never told him that his powers would shut off, but the next morning his powers were off. He survived for the next 20 years.

When he was 40 years old he went to the continent of Africa. He moved because he got busted by a policeman for putting up a stop sign and some flowers in response to police brutality, and so he went to jail for 20 years.

When he was 60 years old, he got so disappointed that he looked for a savior. That savior came from out of nowhere; a genius scientist that could help Jefferson.

The scientist's name was Little Einstein. He took Jefferson out of jail and put him in a cage. Jefferson shouted, "No!"

The scientist exclaimed, "Stop moving. I am going to help you!"

"Never!"

"Stop, OK?" asked the scientist.

"OK," Jefferson answered.

The scientist zapped him. He had a laser that could bring back your life, and in about 158 hours it turned Jefferson back to human. He touched his body and realized that there was no fur on it! Jefferson was so happy.

It helped him to have a better life, until he was 95 years old.

He got so rich that he was like a leprechaun with a pot of gold. He behaved nicely since he became human with a lot of money. Five years later, when Jefferson was 100 years old, it was his last night on Earth.

He started to give away his mansion and cool cars for free.

When it was 1:00 P.M., he slept and rested in peace.

Things on Earth looked all black to Jefferson, and he was doing a lot of resting in peace at the funeral. Everyone was so sad that they couldn't say anything funny at the funeral like a chatterbox or a clown would, but they gave stuff to Jefferson to tell him that they loved him.

But then, at 1:30 P.M., Jefferson faked his death! He breathed in his casket. He had just been drinking potions to make him sleep.

He started running like a cheetah on the highway, at a ferocious speed. He was free.

The Fluffy Cloud

by MARY STEINHOFF

ne night, up in the magical place of a million stars in outer space, Pink Fluff Trial was making colorful fluffles with stars. This is how they make a new monster. They rolled a big ball of fur together to make a monster called Fluffle. She was a regular, pink monster with a cat tail, who always made horns and danced on rainbows. She was sent down to Earth because Fluffle Trial wanted to spy on the people down on Earth.

I went to play outside one day and I saw a pink, fluffy ball. I touched it and Fluffle popped out! She was so nice that I wanted her to be my pet. Now that she was my pet, she started to make a home full of fur in my closet when I went to school.

But when I got home from school she was gone! Fluffle was back in space getting a crystal made out of warmth and rainbows. She battled Evil Dr. Porkchop, too. He looks like a pig wearing a top hat. He is a bad guy because he stole bacon from the Fluffle Trial. They fought and she won the battle by putting glue on the wall and pushing him into it. "Sticky enough for you?" Fluffle said. When she got home, she devoured a cupcake.

That night when I went to bed, Fluffle's blanket was as colorful as a rainbow with crystals in the sunlight. I was super happy to see her. The next morning we ate some cereal and Fluffle and I went into the closet to play in the fur. It was amazing.

Then, Evil Dr. Porkchop came back! He captured Fluffle by setting a trap that was made out of spikes, so I glued him to the wall and got Fluffle back. I slept over at her fluff house (that is in my closet) and later, we danced. Finally, we went to her fluffy bed and were joyful. I thought to myself that night, *I have the best monster ever.*

The next day we woke up and I was so excited! I was going to Fluffle World. It is up in outer space where Fluffle was born. We went in the afternoon. Her planet was on fire. She was as sad as a crying seal.

I said, "It's OK!"

She sniffed and then she saw the terrible Evil Dr. Porkchop. Fluffle sprang into action and got really mad. She gave Evil Dr. Porkchop the evil stare. Evil Dr. Porkchop gave a scared screech.

"Ahh!" he said, "Sorry."

He cleaned Fluffle World up and then flew away in his piggy blimp that looks just like him. He never bothered them again.

When we got home, Fluffle felt as good as a spring morning. She was filled with joy that her planet was saved. That evening, we played with Rocco (my dog) and for dinner we had tacos, mmmm! Then, I got my PJs on and went to bed with Fluffle. Boy, what a day I had.

The next day we woke up. I said to Fluffle while crunching my cereal, "Doesn't this—*crunch*—cereal taste funny?"

Fluffle started to laugh and said, "That's not cereal—that's cat litter!" so I spit it out and ate ice cream instead. After breakfast/dessert Fluffle said, "Let's have a dance party at Dance Party Planet."

THAT'S NOT CEREAL– THAT'S CAT LITTER!

I said, "Let's do it!" At Dance Party Planet we were dancing and the door opened. Instead of Evil Dr. Porkchop, it was someone new.

It was The Party Pooper and he was half-fish on the back side and half-goat on the front side. He would spit on people or even poop on them. We said his name twice, which made him say, "Hey, that is not funny!" Then he pooped on the party, literally!

I said, "Eww."

He challenged us to a duel, so we all did a nae nae and sang, *Watch me whip, now watch me nae nae*, and we won. We cleaned up the poop and we danced some more. When we went home I said, "Well, time for bed."

Many months later, it was the day Fluffle and I had been waiting for. It was Christmas Eve! I got out of bed quickly, unlike Fluffle. She was still in bed. Anyway, I was hanging up the ornaments on the Christmas tree, making hot chocolate for Santa, baking cookies, and writing my Christmas list. I went to see Fluffle and she looked like she was very ill. I felt her head and it was hot! She was really sick. I did not know how to take care of a sick monster!

Then I started thinking bad thoughts. What if she hated me? If I did not take care of her, what if she died? So I went to bed. I was excited about Christmas but worried about Fluffle. At night, I heard footsteps and Fluffle started turning red and green. She felt so much better.

In the morning, we opened the presents. Fluffle had a present from Santa and it had pink wrapping. I felt so happy, I hugged Fluffle. This was really the best Christmas ever.

The Thing You Love the Most

by AMANDA VASQUEZ

 hree days ago, a conversation happened in the kitchen between a mother and daughter.

"Hey," smiled Mom.

"Hey," grumbled Brenda.

"Want me to make you breakfast?"

"No, I'm good, Mom," she said in a rude way.

Brenda and her mom, Natalie, didn't really get along because Brenda felt like her mom judged her all time, and Natalie thought she was being ridiculous. Brenda was Natalie's only child—at least that's what Brenda thought.

One day, in the kitchen again, Brenda asked her mom, "Can I go to the store?"

"Which one?"

"Chanel," Brenda said.

"Sure, but be back at noon all right?"

"All right."

Brenda left, but Brenda was not going to the store. She was going out with her boyfriend, Steven. Knowing that her mother did not like him, she lied to her. Steven worked at PayPay Shoe Store and Natalie just had a bad feeling about him. He was like a snake that slithered through Brenda's life, and Natalie did not like that.

As she left, Natalie heard footsteps and went to go see who it was, but no one was there. Natalie saw wet footprints on the stairs going upstairs to the rooms.

She went up the steps and asked, "Is someone there?"

The thing making the footsteps said, "Natalie."

The voice was like the screeching wind on a winter's day.

"Who said that?"

"Natalie..."

"Show yourself!"

"No!" the thing said, "I will never."

"Please, stop. Just tell me who you are."

"Never. Come with me."

"No."

But the thing didn't listen to her and kidnapped Natalie to an abandoned warehouse close by. The thing was ghost-like and looked like when the sun hits the window—a beam of tan light that moves quickly but you can never see it move. The thing disappeared and popped up by her and used all its energy to put a pillowcase over her head. The thing possessed her body so she couldn't talk. Natalie had no choice but to do what it said. She tried to fight but she couldn't.

Natalie woke up and saw herself trapped in a chair and saw the thing that had kidnapped her. She wondered how the thing that was now a human-like creature was standing before her. It was a young man in his teen years. He looked tall and had brown eyes and brown hair. He had a scar on his mouth that looked like a little snake.

She asked, "What do you want from me?" She was panting with anger.

"So, you don't know who I am?" the thing accused.

"No."

"I am your son, Jake."

Natalie was shocked to see him.

"Why do you look so dismayed?" Jake asked.

"Because I left you when you were little, and now you're so big . . . And now, you're a . . . ghost?"

"Why did you leave me? You left me thinking all this time that I was not the little boy you wanted me to be . . . for years. And now . . . I'm dead."

Natalie was confused. She always thought she'd done the right thing by placing her son with his Aunt Judy in a safe home. But now the ghost of her son was haunting her with a very serious message.

"No, it's not that. It's just . . . let me explain—" Natalie begged.

"What was it? I will never care what you have to say to me! I had to try, and try, and try to find you and when I did, I saw this little girl with you, Brenda. You were laughing and smiling. I was watching you and her just having a good time, thinking you left me there, just wondering and hoping you would come back, and—"

Natalie interrupted him. "When you were a little boy I couldn't afford you anymore. I tried to keep you but I just couldn't do it." Natalie started to cry. "When you were about five years old, Aunt Judy came to see you for the first time. We started to talk about everything and she suggested that she should take you into her hands, and when I got everything taken care of I could come get you. So I took the deal, but I messed up! I thought she lived by Largett's Home Store at 2844 N. Walk Street, but—"

"So you messed up like always. She never took me in and I was living on the streets!"

"Yeah but after that—"

"Stop, I don't want to hear anymore."

Jake lived on the streets because Aunt Judy never picked him from the foster care facility. One night, when he was about 12, he opened the window, jumped onto a tree, climbed down, and ran away into the streets of Chicago! That was the day he saw his mom with another little girl, happy, and he was haunted by what he had seen that day.

Days later, Jake was feeling depressed, like gray smoke floating around through the skies, and he wasn't paying attention while walking. The light went green—and a car didn't see him and hit him. When the car crashed into him, he changed instantly into a black-hooded ghost with evil light.

Jake left Natalie there, sobbing.

After just a few minutes passed, Natalie realized that Jake had left his phone on the table. She saw the rope tied on her and tried to escape like eight times. Finally, she got through the rope. She got up and called 9-1-1 but then she heard Jake's footsteps, so she dropped the rope behind her and continued to cry so that Jake wouldn't think she was planning her escape.

"Stop crying," he said in an annoyed voice.

"I can't! I was such a bad mother, please just let me go."

"No, you are just going to tell the police, plus I just came to get my phone and give you a message: *The thing you love the most is not what you think it is. It's with the shedding skin of a snake.*

"But like I said, I'm also just here to find my phone. Where is my phone? I must have left it in the other room," he said, but as he was leaving the tan light beamed through him and shifted him to another room.

Just as he started to shift, he heard, "9-1-1—what's your emergency?"

He shifted back in the room and saw Natalie untangle from the ropes with the phone in her hand. He said, "What was that?"

"I don't know what you're talking about."

"Give it to me."

"No."

"Now!"

"No." Natalie tried to grab his hand but her hand slipped through him. He looked back and tried to shift her off of him. She said, "Wait. What do you really want from me?"

What Jake wanted—more than anything—was for him to connect and be loved by his family.

The emergency crew arrived and when Natalie heard the loud sirens she was relieved. They entered the warehouse quickly and went to help Natalie, but Jake heard them and blended in with the tan sun beams through the window. Natalie looked around and was all alone and confused. She tried to explain to the crew what had happened, but no one believed her. She was all alone with the ghost of her son and all she could think about was whether or not Brenda was hurt.

The emergency crew put a blanket around Natalie's shoulders and called Brenda to make sure she was OK. The crew reported that Brenda was with Steven, finished with shopping and OK. But Natalie was not convinced.

What did her son, the ghost, really mean? She couldn't get the image of a snake out of her mind.

Ben the Big, Burly Monster

by ERIC BUSTAMANTE

My monster's name is Ben, a name given to him by God. It means "big and burly" because Ben is strong.

Ben was born on March 10th, 1002, in Clown Town. He lives in a cold, harsh basement and sleeps on the hardwood floor without a blanket because he can't afford one.

My monster was a regular man once. Now, people make fun of him. In retaliation, he throws food at them. Ben likes to scare people with his face because it is ghostly white. He has nasty, smelly, matted fur that you can find bugs in, and that scares people. He uses his long, filthy fingernails to eat the bugs.

Ben likes to hit and swing at people because he likes to see them in pain. He hates people who cry because he hates the noise. Ben gets around by stealing quiet red motorcycles because they are fast and easy to hide from the cops.

Ben lays down to relax and he falls asleep quickly. When he sleeps, he dreams about having a better life with better friends—as a matter of fact, actually having friends. He really wishes to have a friend, so he sleeps a lot to dream of them.

The Uninvited Guest

by VIKTOR MLADENOV

Last night when I got home, I thought I saw a meteor crashing into the forest. I went in to see what had happened and I saw a little rock. I gasped, thinking the little rock looked like an egg, and I was correct. I saw a little creature coming out from the egg.

I picked it up and said, "Hello little creature, I am going to name you Stichi."

He was light green with two hands of green poofy fur, and each hand had three fingers. He had two thick legs with long flowing fur, and four toes with short nails. He was as small as a baby. Stichi had a long, brown tail with black dots on it and he had small, sharp teeth. I went to my mom and asked, "Can we keep it?"

My mom yelled, "No!"

I was mad, so I hid Stichi in my room. The next day when I got home from school, I saw that my mom was still at work. I went to my room and saw Stichi had scratched holes in the walls and made drawings that looked like his parents. I was mad as a wildcat stuck in a cage, so I called my friend Ethan over to my house to see if he wanted to help. He came to my house and we cleaned up, but had no idea what to do with the walls. My face was red as lava. Stichi had something in his hands and I picked it up. It looked like an alien weapon or something. I hid it somewhere he couldn't find it. The walls were white, so we used white tape to hide the holes. But that wouldn't last forever.

The next day when I got home from school, I saw something that looked really scary: a dog's face, six long hands, and a long dragon tail that was red all over. The monster was trying to kidnap Stichi, but I did not run away.

When I came near it I said, "Let him go, you ugly monster!"

The ugly monster shouted, "Nooo, haha!"

His breath smelled like he had been eating garbage. Suddenly, he pulled Stichi so hard that I let go of him. The ugly monster ran away, but I remembered that alien spear that Stichi had, so I grabbed it. Then, immediately, I ran to see where the ugly monster had gone. After 10 minutes of searching, I saw it running in the forest.

I ran to the monster and said, "Freeze!"

The monster gasped back, "OMG, don't hurt me!" He was scared as a cat running from a dog. I told him to give me Stichi back or I would throw the spear, but I wasn't really going to aim at him. He gave me Stichi. I was happy as a millionaire.

I yelled to the monster, "Get out, and never come back!"

The monster gasped, "OK!"

Stichi and I ran back to the house. I ordered pepperoni pizza over the phone and called Ethan over to my house. We were happy that it was all over.

The next day I saw Stichi going somewhere and followed him to see where he was going. I saw some creatures that looked like his parents because they looked like Stichi, but just older and as big as a five-year-old kid. I felt really happy that I saw Stichi's parents. Stichi saw me and hugged me. Stichi then went to his parents and got inside their machine. I think it was a UFO or something.

"Bye, Stichi, bye."

I wasn't that sad because he and his parents were together again. I am mostly happy that he is OK. Sometimes, on my way home from school, I remember how we said bye to each other, and I get kind of sad. And sometimes, when I go to sleep, I remember Stichi. And sometimes, I wish that Stichi would come back to say hi to me someday.

OMG!

Bella's Loco Trip

by KIANA GRAYER

POSTED AT 8:08 AM

ella, a 13-year-old monster, lives in a fairy hotel. She was born in a ginger-bread house. (I, Kiana, am typing this because Bella is at her gingerbread house for Christmas). Bella sleeps in a tiny, clear bubble so if a stranger comes, she can quickly float away.

On the outside, Bella has blonde, wavy hair, blue eyes, and pale skin (but not white-pale). On the inside she is sweet and fun. She has all the superpowers in the world, so she's prepared for anything. She can speak to me by mind. She flies all the time and likes to do flips. To get places quicker, she rides in a limo.

Bella has many secrets. One of them is that she can turn into a ghost. She's terrified of Evil Bacon taking over the world. He's a short and fuzzy spirit that makes burnt bacon and is the worst person ever. Evil Bacon once got into President Lilly's body and kept making her slap herself!

POSTED AT 3:03 PM

Bella took a vacation to Washington D.C. On the plane, she screamed, "I'm so excited!" as she was kicking in her seat.

When she got there, she got a hot dog, chips, ice cream, and watermelon. She was hungry from her plane trip. She decided to visit the president, Lilliana Maria Harris. When she got to the White House, she rang the pure-gold doorbell.

President Lilly sang, "May I help you?" as Bella took another bite of her hot dog.

Bella mumbled, "I was wondering if I could take a few pictures."

President Lilly was in a terrible mood. She yelled "NO!" in Evil Bacon's voice. She yelled that in that evil, grumpy, grim, low tone because, whenever President Lilly gets mad, she turns into the short and furry Evil Bacon. She was so upset to be bothered that President Lilly sent Bella to jail. She also took Bella's powers away by putting a spell on her, using a wand she found in the garbage. The spell went, *Change, change, take your powers away.*

Bella yelled, "Dang it!" as her powers disappeared.

President Lilly, still mad, shouted, "Be quiet!"

President Lilly forgot to take Bella's phone when she locked her up. Bella called her mom—who had blonde hair and always wore wedges. Bella remembered a spell that could break her out! She said, *"Open, open when you say: 'spoon.'"*

Bella's mom whispered, "Spoon."

The lock popped open, and Bella got her powers back! She croaked, "I'm never going to Washington D.C. again!" Bella yelled.

When Bella got home, she and her mom went to see a movie which was about the exact same thing that happened to Bella.

"This is a coincidence, right?" whispered Bella.

That night, it was all over the news that Evil Bacon had gotten into President Lilly's brain and made her eat poisonous bacon. Evil Bacon was destroyed and President Lilly fainted. The president did not die, but she wasn't allowed to be president anymore, because she put a person in jail for asking a question.

But those were the old days—now, new adventures are waiting.

Mighty and the Three Kids

by OSCAR MONRREAL

ILLUSTRATOR: LYDIA FU / STUDENT: AMANDA VASQUEZ, PAGE 160

This is the story of a lifetime, starting in the village called Dullahan Village. The village was a kingdom ruled by a king. The village was made up of brick houses, a forest, mountains, and a huge waterfall. The village was like a festival, full of decorations, pearls, crystals, and jewelry. All of the Dullahans were half-man, half-horse, with no heads. They wore decorations like rings, headbands, bracelets, and necklaces. All the jewelry gave them great powers like magic defense, magic attack, and magic strength. They were fearless.

The king's son, Mighty, was so different that none of the Dullahans wanted him anymore. Mighty had once challenged three kids named Jared, Nyne, and Carly. He tried to defeat them, but he lost the fight. Jared had spiky hair that was dyed red and wore a shirt with a symbol for peace on it. He was adventurous and curious and he'd never give up on anything. Nyne had neat, well-kept hair that was light brown. He always wore shorts and a shirt with a symbol for curiosity on it, and he was good at climbing rocks. Carly had beautiful long, black hair, and wore a dress that flowed in the wind. She also wore pearls and a headband that was black but patterned with leaves like a princess. Jared and Nyne thought she was beautiful and always full of happiness.

One day, mysterious creatures came to Dullahan Village and attacked. Everyone was like, "I've never seen this creature before."

The king called out, "Attack!" and Mighty came to accept his challenge. He started to fight with swords. Mighty made the last attack and wounded the enemy's shoulder. The creatures' dirty-faced leader cried, "Arghhhhhhh! I've never seen anyone fight like this!"

And off they went. The enemy leader went away, and people were cheering for Mighty.

His father was impressed, and he made Mighty a knight to protect people.

The next day, his father and Mighty were sitting together. His father said, "You did great out there, son. You protected our village." Mighty thanked his father. Then his father bid him good night.

"Good night, Dad," Mighty replied.

When Mighty went to sleep, his darkened room filled with dark spirits flying around. They went inside Mighty's head. The next day, when Mighty woke up for lunch, he was talking in a scary voice, saying that all the Dullahans should be banished forever!

His father replied, "How dare you? This is how you repay me? You are kicked out of this village. Leave! Leave this instant!"

It was a harsh punishment, but hearing that the Dullahans would be banished had filled Mighty's father with fear. All the Dullahans were super angry and upset. The Dullahans scolded, "You are a disgrace to your father! Mighty, why would you do this? We're very disappointed, Mighty. Leave. You are banned from this village forever."

When he tried to return, the other Dullahans just looked at him. They exclaimed, "Go away. Remember, you've been banned from this village."

Then, Mighty made an announcement that he wanted forgiveness. He told his people that he was sorry because something was controlling his head, making him do what he did to his father.

The Dullahans responded, "No," so Mighty cried and ran away.

He had nothing to eat or drink, but he still had his jewelry. He made fire. He had no comfort, he had no father, and something was happening to his brain. He got insanely crazy. He went out of control. He was not feeling good, and he was acting like something else—all of his body had changed. His eyes changed color, and his DNA changed. He had a headache and was complaining that his head hurt. His skin and his whole body were in pain.

Meanwhile, Jared, Nyne, and Carly heard a voice say, "Swallow these light spheres," so the kids swallowed some blue spheres they'd found. Something weird was happening. Their throats were burning and their shadows were different. Three mythical shadow creatures came out of their shadows. Nyne's was a tiger, Carly's was a gecko, and Jared's was a bearded dragon. Now, the kids had even more magic and powers.

They left on a journey to get back to Snowflake Village, a village full of wooden houses and a wooden bridge. The village had a lot of snow and windmills. On the way, a giant lizard that was tied to a rope made them fall into a tunnel and into some ancient ruins. Nyne noticed something: a dark cave full with treasures and mythical creatures. They discussed that the place looked familiar, and Jared said, "Yes, this is the ancient ruins, full of treasures and creatures like Poo Snake."

Nyne was trying to explain the place to the others, and Carly was scared that the ancient ruins could be dangerous. In the ruins they met this creature who was a half-robin, half-human and wore a blue shirt. His legs were covered with feathers and his name was Bird Boy. Together, they joined forces and were more powerful. Together, they traveled all the way to their families.

Then, they saw something coming, and you know who it was? It was Mighty, running to those three kids. Mighty again accepted their challenge to fight, and the three kids used magic—all different kinds of magic. Mighty was using his sword and his power of Earth's realm. Mighty tried to beat them, but they were too powerful. Mighty started getting weaker and weaker because the three kids had been upgrading their magic with the light spheres.

Mighty was defeated and thwarted by the three kids. The three kids cheered for their victory.

Back in the Dullahan Village, the Dullahans were sad and crying about Mighty, because they hadn't seen him for a long time. They missed him after he was banished.

Meanwhile, inside the house, The King was watching the news and he heard that Mighty was dead. Mighty's dad shouted, "Noooooooooooooo! Mighty, I am so sorry."

The king made an announcement that Mighty was dead, and all Dullahans gasped and cried, saying, "Mighty was a great man, we're so sorry."

The king decided that the Dullahans should walk into the waterfall as a tribute to Mighty, since that was how Dullahans showed that they were in mourning. One by one, the Dullahans walked through the waterfall, and once the last one passed through, the entrance to their village became magically sealed.

To this day, the waterfall is still known as the Waterfall of Sadness.

The Pegaphix

by VLADIMIR ARROYO

 long time ago in Australia, there was a Pegaphix named Frank who was five years old. He lived in the desert around towns where there was stuff to eat, like fruits and farm veggies. He was born in a volcano not far from the town. He slept on the edges of caves, so the sun hit him but he didn't get wet. It seemed like he was a mean guy since he was always on fire, but he was actually nice.

He could fly like a Pegasus and turn his fire on and off. He could talk in full human sentences and he usually shook his head when he got mad and jumped when he got excited. He got around with his mighty fire wings, soaring like an eagle, but he turned into a rock if you threw dirt on top of him. All he wanted was a friend, and he had a habit of playing pranks on villagers. He loved villagers but hated hunters and poachers as much as a kid was afraid of clowns. He got very angry when someone put out his fire, and he relaxed by turning off his fire and letting the sun hit him. He was most afraid of dirt because it could turn him solid, and he couldn't move until someone broke him out of his rock shell.

One day, Frank the Pegaphix was playing video games in his fiery volcano like a kid during the weekend, and he wanted to go to the village. Frank went to the village and started to cool down before he got there, but he touched some hay and set it on fire. He quickly dashed away so the villagers would suspect that one of their lamps fell and set the grass on fire.

The next morning, he came back, but he first started cooling down right when he left so he wouldn't burn anything. But when he got there, the villagers ran him out as fast as racing horses, all except for an eight-year-old kid named Bob.

The townfolk hollered, "That brute must never come back! Sooner or later we won't even have a town if that monstrosity keeps incinerating our houses. They will all be turned to ashes."

That kid didn't want to run him out because he knew he didn't mean to light the hay on fire. So the kid walked away from the town to find the Pegaphix. He couldn't find him, until he finally saw a faint light in a cave on the mountain side.

He followed the light.

There was the Pegaphix, sleeping. He touched the Pegaphix and burned his hand. When the boy screamed and woke up Frank, his fire lit up like a firework.

The boy ran out of the cave in terror.

Frank whispered, "Are you OK, Bob?"

Frank didn't mean to scare him, so he took the boy back to his town.

There in the town square, the boy tried to convince the people in town that the Pegaphix was a good guy.

"He won't burn the town down if you just treat him equally."

"He will still burn it down. He's made of fire."

The town didn't accept it. So they started to throw food like tomatoes, carrots, lettuce, and—Frank's worst nightmare—spinach. The Pegaphix got really mad. His flame heated up and he burned some straw. It started burning the town. When the Pegaphix saw that, he started trying to put out the fire.

"Oh no, I've got to put out this fire. I would appreciate help."

"He's right. We need to help if we don't want our town to burn."

The villagers saw. They also started to help put out the fire instead of screaming and running around town.

They finally put out the fire.

The town didn't hate the Pegaphix any more, and they had a celebration for him putting out the fire. The party had a cake and lasted until 5:00 A.M.

After the party, there was a ceremony at midnight to name Frank the town hero. At the ceremony they gave him a golden medallion that said "Town Savior"!

Frank the Pegaphix treasured that golden medallion forever. All the people in the town became his friends. All the kids played with him every day.

Jim the Monster

by SPARKLES FELICIANO

im is 100 years old. He is a nice, big monster. He is black and his eyes are green. His teeth are big and red. He lives in a dark, cold cave and sleeps on top of a rock. He was born in a hospital. He is so nice and not mean to anybody.

He is in a car going somewhere to have fun.

At night, Jim's power is his glowing eyes. They let him see and get food to eat for dinner. He loves it.

Jim fears people and he dreams to be free. He loves little kids and he hates groups. He is sad when a big kid runs away from him.

Jim relaxes on an old couch, and that's good enough for him.

Jim's mom's name is Jimm. She is intimidated by Big Bug the Heart.

When Jimm's baby boy, Jim, was happy, she loved him. Another monster was mad when Jimm's baby got big.

When Jim was 12 years old, that monster was so mad that he took Jim and his mom. Jim escaped, but his mom was gone, so he looked for her.

The police monster found Jimm. She was tired, but she was so happy because she was with her boy again.

Fluffy and Bethsaida

by BETHSAIDA CRUZ

luffy was a bad monster who had brown fur with black eyes and yellow paws. She always wore a sparkly bow tie. She went to school like a regular girl because her best friend Bethsaida had begged the principal. At school, Fluffy was a bully to other people. She said bad things about them. Once, in the lunchroom, Fluffy told a little girl, "Give me your lunch." The little girl was eating pasta, which Fluffy loved.

The little girl was so scared that she gave away her lunch. But later, Fluffy felt bad about what she was doing. She asked herself, "Why am I doing this?"

At home in her apartment she decided that she would say sorry to the people she'd bullied. Fluffy walked up to a girl in her class she'd once told, "I am better than you."

"I'm sorry I told you I was better than you," Fluffy cried. The girl said it was okay. And the others said it was okay, too.

Fluffy was trying to find a place that was quiet because her head hurt a lot and she wanted to lie down for a little bit. She had thought so much about how mean she was that it hurt her head.

Fluffy escaped to her secret hiding place. She had her own house that was a two hour bus ride away. It had a big back yard with many flowers in the front. There were sunflowers, and pretty red and white roses. The outside of the house was darkish and lightish red. The house was much bigger inside than it looked outside. Fluffy loved the little blue hallways and her angel decorations. She said, "It's quiet here. It's peaceful here."

Suddenly, Fluffy's best friend, Bethsaida, entered the secret house and the room where Fluffy was relaxing.

"Why are you lying down?" asked Bethsaida.

"I'm going to sleep," exclaimed Fluffy.

"Goodnight, Fluffy," whispered Bethsaida. Then she discovered an extra bed and also took a nap.

Two hours later, Fluffy went for a walk, looking for something to cure her boredom. It was now night, and Fluffy left while Bethsaida was sleeping. But Bethsaida saw the bedroom door closing and tracks leading outside.

Where are you, Fluffy? wondered Bethsaida.

Fluffy came home and tried to escape because she didn't want to take a shower, which she knew she'd have to. During the walk, Fluffy had fallen in the mud. Fluffy said she would rather get dirty than take a shower. Having searched outside, Bethsaida could not get back in the house, so she rang the doorbell. Fluffy pretended she was not home and did not get the door. Bethsaida just went ahead and climbed into the house through Fluffy's open window. She saw Fluffy watching TV. Bethsaida snuck up on her.

"I didn't escape," said Fluffy.

She ran to the stairs and tried to jump to the window, but missed. "This is just my hiding spot when I'm bored," she pleaded.

"Didn't you hear me?" asked Bethsaida. "I said it was time to take a shower."

Fluffy just went ahead and took the shower. Bethsaida had told her that if she didn't, she'd throw her lucky coin in the garbage.

In the morning Fluffy saw Bethsaida on the couch watching a movie, *My Babysitter's a Vampire*. Fluffy asked, "Can I watch it, too?"

Fluffy sat next to Bethsaida to watch the movie and when Fluffy got scared, she hugged Bethsaida. Fluffy and Bethsaida kept living in the secret house. They were happy living in a house and not in an apartment where they had to pay rent. Now they could do whatever they wanted: parties without asking, making a mess, or watering the flowers.

The Rise of Broryx

by ETHAN VEGA

roryx was on Saturn when he had his first banana. He did not like it because it tasted old.

"I will destroy all bananas," Broryx yelled. Bananas ended up on Saturn when astronauts were flying by and their bananas flew out of the aircraft each time one of the astronauts pushed a release button.

There were three crates of bananas. Broryx was walking and saw one banana and ate it.

"Build a rocket to blow up Earth where the bananas come from!" He told his servants.

They worked on the rocket day and night, but then Broryx echoed, "Everyone on Saturn must try bananas because they need to see if they like it or not like it."

A few of them liked the bananas. Then they finished the rocket. The rocket was large and deadly, with 500 pounds of banana bombs attached to it! So then Broryx was going to launch it but then Blaze came.

Blaze said to Broryx, "Why won't you just destroy the bananas that came here?"

Broryx yelled, "No, I will destroy Earth because I don't want them to end up here again!"

Blaze duplicated himself like a shadow because he had a device called "The Duplicator." Meanwhile, Broryx called his army.

A war happened on Saturn. Broryx lost lots of his soldiers and Blaze did, too. Broryx did not fight because the rocket's engine broke down and Broryx was not able to repair it. His servants had passed from Blaze shadows. They used lasers that are red and blue for the good and bad side!

After a day or two, Blaze found a cannon near a mountain. The cannon was old and rusty but it still functioned. Blaze was thinking of something to do with his last banana. Yes! He put a fresh and new banana in the cannon and shot it! He aimed for Broryx's mouth. A banana went in his mouth.

Boryx yelled, "Now I love bananas!" The bananas that landed on Saturn were sour like an old lemon.

Broryx and Blaze went down to Earth. They both bought banana splits with fudge, vanilla ice cream, and nuts on it. It tasted like fresh bananas and chocolate ice cream, and it was crunchy. Broryx and Blaze bought all the bananas on the Earth and Broryx renamed Saturn "Banana Planet"!

Next Blaze had to leave. Broryx wanted him to stay, but Blaze protects planets, and had to go. Broryx gave Blaze five crates of bananas and they said goodbye. Broryx stored all of Earth's bananas in a really, really, really big vault with a password, fingerprint code, and voice recognition which was impossible to steal. Broryx shared bananas all over Banana Planet, but was sad that Blaze left. Then, Broryx saw a ship in deep space. There was someone looking through a telescope.

Broryx was really happy to see Blaze again. Broryx and Blaze became rulers of Banana Planet! Blaze said to Broryx, "I'm sorry I left. It's my duty to patrol planets but I'll stop that and be a co-leader."

Humans from Earth came to the planet for bananas, because all of Earth's bananas were gone. Banana Planet was now a dome with some trees so the humans could survive and not die, and a place for astronauts to take a break, eat, and refill their oxygen. Broryx and Blaze were the most important people in space because they had a rest stop for astronauts.

Luna and the Battle for Preservation

by VANESSA BENAVIDES

F ar away, there was once a sea kingdom named Benzo that was made out of rare gems. The gems were black opals that were really pretty, because they had all the rainbow colors in them. It looked like a rainbow universe! The kingdom was also made out of clams made of abalone shells, which are really shiny.

The kingdom was full of beautiful galaxy stones. The galaxy stones made the kingdom really pop. The kingdom was as valuable as a million diamonds. People fought to own it.

"It's mine!" people would yell.

"No, it's mine!" other people would shriek back.

In the kingdom lived lots of mermaids. The chosen one, the special one, was Luna, but she just didn't know it. Luna always wore a necklace that was really special, because not only did it help her keep her powers, but her mom gave it to her when she was a baby. She had worn it ever since.

Luna's power was love. She could also turn into a human and go to the human world on land—Luna called it the Magical World, but she'd never been there. Luna had 21 other siblings. She actually had 22 other siblings, but she didn't know she had an extra sibling. She always loved it when somebody said the word "love" or when people fell in love!

One day, Luna went on an adventure and found a necklace that read *Luna and Venus*. Luna right away thought, *Who is this person called Venus?*

Luna took the necklace and told her dad, Martian. Her dad had no answer and kept quiet. Luna kept pleading with her dad to tell her, but he wouldn't budge.

Over time, Luna got madder and madder, and more curious.

"Don't do it, Luna. Curiosity killed the cat!" her family would say.

Eventually, Luna ran away to find out who Venus was.

All the other mermaids got together with Luna's dad and sent out a search party to try to find her.

Luna searched for days and months until she found what she was looking for.

On Luna's journey, she met a friendly fish named Bubbles. They got so attached that Bubbles followed her on the rest of the journey.

And then she found it, in the middle of nowhere. For Luna, finding the cave was as hard as learning how to drive, since she'd never been to the Magical World.

"Finally, a cave that actually looks warm and cozy! I hope that there aren't any Sea Guardians inside," Luna muttered as she slowly got ready to attack.

Luna didn't want there to be Sea Guardians because they were meanies! They were a clan that protected really deep, hidden caves in case anything suspicious happened. Luckily, there weren't any Sea Guardians inside.

Luna had been trying to find a cave to sleep in during the night. When she entered the cave, it was dark, and somehow someone had enchanted the cave so it could look like a normal cave.

Luna saw a girl who had an evil fish friend named Mr. Pufferstein. The girl was all red—she looked really creepy with her red eyes, red hair, and red fire dress. Mr. Pufferstein was as evil as an old penny-pinching, fire-breathing dragon.

The girl said, "Puff, go get me the fairy. Soon, Benzo will be mine! MWAHAHAHA-HAHAHA!"

Puff said, "Yes, master Venus."

Meanwhile, as this conversation was going on, Luna was camouflaged behind a rock. She was shocked. Puff had responded "Venus."

But how was this possible? The girl's name was Venus!

Venus also said, "Then I'll get Luna!"

Luna got up from behind the rock and said, "Hey! I'm the one you want."

Luna shot a love spell to make her acceptable again. The spell was supposed to make Venus good again, but Venus dodged the spell and shot a spell to Luna. Luna fell, but it didn't harm her. Meanwhile, Puff was fighting with Bubbles. Puff used to be Bubbles' best friend when they were small, but he was tricked into joining the evil group, a.k.a. the Deadly Finns.

Anyway, this fighting went on forever, until Venus shouted, "Nobody can stop me from ruling the King—"

Venus was about to finish what she said, but Luna interrupted and exclaimed, "*Love is good, as sweet as can be, don't forget to make this person good again!*"

Luna shot the love spell and Venus fell to the ground, lying unconscious. She was unconscious for five months. When she finally woke up she looked different, and she was exceptional.

Venus had blue, wavy hair that sparkled, a flowery outfit that matched, and light blue eyes.

Venus woke up, afraid of her surroundings. Venus told Luna everything about how she turned evil. She explained, "I was tricked by the Deadly Finns! They gave me a drink that made me do everything they would say!"

Luna gasped at the news.

Venus responded, "It was terrible!"

Luna said, "I can't imagine all that you've been through!"

They welcomed Venus back to Benzo by throwing a parade. Martian welcomed Venus by giving her tons of gifts. Luna felt very happy Venus was back. She had never met her before, and she was happy to welcome someone new to her family.

The Million Dollar Monster

by AMARIS REYES

tch was a monster who looked like a blue, fluffy koala. He was as short as a 3-year-old and had two eyes and four hands, but those other two hands were hiding so he appeared like a normal person. Itch went to Monster School, which is a college for the teenagers and adults who need help in school, and where Itch learned how to scare people and how to lose weight. Monster School is a castle that's inside of a school and has lots of candy and bubblegum.

After Monster School one day, Itch went to call J-Ber to get Munkin Ponuts. He was craving *dice cream* and *mash browns*. When it was evening, Itch went to Bony's to get groceries because Itch had a date with Pitch. She had long, beautiful hair and she was also hiding two of her hands. She was a pink, fluffy koala and she was fat and soft, like Itch. Outside, there was a lottery box. Itch went to get a lottery ticket. When Itch scratched it off, he won $12,000,000. Itch screamed from the top of his lungs, "THIS IS THE BEST DAY OF MY LIFE!"

Itch went straight to the Mapple store and tried to ask the boss if he could fire everyone, but the boss asked, "Why do you need to fire everyone?"

Itch answered by saying, "I need to have this Mapple store as a house because my family doesn't like Itch House."

The next morning, Itch got a pumpkin spice latte at Larbucks. After Larbucks, Itch went back to the Mapple store and told the boss, "Can I give you $10,000 for the Mapple store, please?"

"You made yourself a deal, but first you need to pick two people to be your maid and your butler."

They started kicking everybody out except two workers, Juan and Gabby, who volunteered to work and help Itch.

Itch said, "Juan, do you want a cup of tea?"

"No thank you."

"Gabby, do you want a cup of tea to relax?"

"Oh, yes, please," said Gabby. Itch wanted to be nice to them. He wanted them to relax a little because they had been working a lot and maybe they were tired.

Soon after, Itch had an idea to sing and do viral videos.

Itch went outside and asked, "Juan, Gabby, can you please set up a background so I can do a viral video and sing?"

"Yeah, that's a good idea! Right, Juan?"

"Yeah, Gabby, that's a great idea," Juan echoed.

Gabby exclaimed, "So, what are waiting for? Let's get to work, Juan!"

"Awesome! I'm ready!" Juan shouted.

Over the next two weeks, Itch went viral with his music and dance videos. Itch got married to Pitch and had two adorable kids, and Juan and Gabby were babysitters.

Itch got famous and went to the red carpet to watch a movie premiere because he had gotten one million views.

FRIENDS FOREVER

Annabeth and the
Death-Eating Ghost

by L.M. HARRIS

e open our a story on the night before Halloween, in a cemetery in New York City where there was once a ghost named Annabeth. Annabeth had long, dark brown hair and wore an ankle-length white sleeping gown that went down to her toes. Annabeth was planning on leaving her grave on Halloween night, because that is the only time she could leave. Her plan was to find a house where there were children trick-or-treating. And once she found her victim, she would take him to be her "forever friend."

When midnight struck, she went to all of the different ghosts to brag about her plan. Every year, the ghosts have parties to celebrate their freedom. Ghosts were listening to a song called "We're Free." They were doing the monster shuffle, eating chicken, ribs, deer, and more meat, and drinking ectoplasm. But really Annabeth didn't celebrate, mostly because she was excited, and because she wanted to get some sleep to save her energy for later. All the ghosts were bugging her about joining, so she stood to eat and then went to back sleep.

The rest of the ghosts were watching "funny movies," but funny movies for them were horror movies. Three o'clock in the morning came, and Annabeth woke up because the ghosts were laughing so loud. In the movie, a woman went into her closet because she was woken up by a loud thud noise. When she opened the closet doors, a horrible monster snatched her into another dimension. The ghosts found that very funny. Annabeth didn't like watching horror movies. Usually, Annabeth read some books when she was bored. When she could go out of the cemetery, she wanted to get a tablet like a Kindle Fire to read more books. Her superpower was to read five books in one day. She could also make cartoons come to life.

The ghosts finished their movie at 3:45 A.M., and they all decided to PARTY! Annabeth made *The Amazing World of Darwin* come to life, because the ghosts begged her so they could party with the cartoons.

At 4:30 A.M., they all crashed out: ghosts on tables, in trees, and on the floor with chicken bones coming out of their mouths, sleeping.

When they were sleeping, Annabeth left the cemetery. She was not allowed, but what did she care? She was already dead. So she went to the park. She thought about why she couldn't make friends easily. So she decided to change herself—not her look, but her image.

When she came back to the cemetery, the ghosts were screaming and saying, "No NOOOOOO!" They were running and flying around like they'd seen a death-eating ghost.

Annabeth said, "What's wrong?" They *did* see a death-eating ghost. Mael-Paexinus was his nickname. Every 50 years Mael-Paexinus would awaken and he would be super duper hungry.

His power was fire, and he was ENORMOUS! He would steal ghosts to store in a dark pit. Annabeth and the rest of the ghosts were flipping out. Mael-Paexinus was from the 1800s, and he had a brown hat, brown leather jacket, and dark black pants. He had long black hair to his shoulders and a scary, dirty face. So of course they were scared of him. But Annabeth left because she wasn't going to let an old ghost get in the way of her big plans.

Annabeth went out of the cemetery and into the park. She met a girl named Kiana Nutty Nutty Pecan. Kiana had brown hair and wore it to the side in a ponytail.

When they saw each other, they introduced themselves and Annabeth sighed, "I have a hard time making friends."

Kiana sniffled, "Me too. People think I'm weird because I read *Captain Monsterpants* even though it's awesome!" That made them realize they weren't so different.

Annabeth laughed, "That seems pretty cool."

They talked for hours (OK, an hour), and became friends. Annabeth learned that you don't need to take children to be your friends. You have to make your own friends. Annabeth didn't know why Kiana was in the park at 4:30 A.M., and Kiana didn't say.

So Annabeth asked, "Why are you in the park at 4:30 in the morning?"

Kiana said, "Me and my mom had a huge fight on what to eat for dinner, so I stomped all the way to my room, locked my bedroom door, thought about it, and ran away."

At 5:00 A.M., Annabeth told Kiana about the death-eating ghost. They headed back to the cemetery where Mael-Paexinus was destroying everything.

Kiana said fearfully, "OK, bye!" but Annabeth grabbed her arm and pulled her back. They stepped up to Mael-Paexinus and she shouted, "Stop destroying everything!"

He replied, like a smarty pants, "What is it to you?"

Annabeth said, "This is my home. Why do you have to be so angry?"

Mael-Paexinus said, "Because I'm Mael-Paexinus!"

Annabeth grabbed Kiana's hand. She said to Kiana, "The power of friendship can break him!"

Annabeth knew that Mael-Paexinus hated friendships. Many ghosts tried to stop him, but when they did Mael-Paexinus quickly got rid of them. Annabeth and Kiana grabbed each other's hands, so did the rest of the ghosts, and they chanted, "*FRIENDS FOREVER FRIENDS FOREVER FRIENDS FOREVER!*" That broke him.

Mael-Paexinus screamed, "NNNNNNNNNNOOOOOOOOOOO!" and his eyes lit up, and so did his mouth. Mael-Paexinus quickly shattered into pieces like broken glass.

After that, the sun came up. Everyone was safe, and they cleaned up everything and stopped the fires. Annabeth told Kiana to go back home to her mom and apologize, and told her, "Next time dinner comes, you go buy Mickey Monald's."

When Kiana got back to her house, there were police cars everywhere. Kiana tapped on her mom's shoulder. Kiana's mom turned around, grabbed and hugged her, and started crying. So did Kiana. Kiana told her mom she met a ghost who had to go back to the cemetery. Of course, Kiana's mom didn't believe her, but she thought it was cute Kiana had imaginary friends, so she let her go back.

Annabeth never took another child again.

About the Teacher

MARK HARLAN is many years old and lives in Chicago. Mark likes following current events and outside activities (even yard work). He is really good at making puns and installing shelves. He wishes that everyone could have unlimited opportunities to try new challenges and visit new places. If he could have any superpower, it would be to have permanent energy. When Mark grows up, he wants to continue to enjoy his family, friends, and career.

About the Authors

ABIGAIL AGUILERA is 10 years old and lives in Chicago. Abigail likes to paint, decorate, bake desserts, and cook different types of foods. She is really good at gymnastics. She wishes she had her own room. If she could have any superpower, it would be superspeed because she could go anywhere she wants. When Abigail grows up, she wants to own a restaurant or fabric store and to find a cure for lupus.

AILANY ARROYO is 10 years old and lives in Chicago. Ailany likes to paint and is really good at bowling. She wishes for a hoverboard and if she could have any superpower, it would be to freeze things. When Ailany grows up, she wants to be an art teacher.

EMILY ARROYO is 10 years old and lives in Chicago. Emily likes art and is really good at basketball. She wishes she could have a hoverboard. If she could have any superpower, it would be to run fast. When Emily grows up, she wants to work for World Wrestling Entertainment (WWE).

VLADIMIR ARROYO is 10 years old and lives in Chicago. Vladimir likes to play adventure games and is really good at origami. He wishes for better handwriting. If he could have any superpower, it would be to control time so whenever he wanted to skip something, he could speed up time to make it pass. When Vladimir grows up, he wants to go to Australia and see each animal there.

ROSA G. ARTEAGA is 11 years old and lives in Chicago. Rosa likes to play basketball and is really good at coloring pictures. If she could have any superpower, it would be flying and transportation because she hates traffic. When Rosa grows up, she wants to be an artist.

VANESSA BENAVIDES is 10 years old and lives in Chicago. Vanessa likes to read fantasy books like Harry Potter and is really good at drawing and making stuff like bows. She wishes: 1. To be Hermione from *Harry Potter* and, 2. To get a hoverboard. If she could have any superpower, it would be to rewind time whenever she makes a wrong choice. When Vanessa grows up, she wants: 1. To be a YouTuber and, 2. To be a movie actress.

BRIELLE LEILANI BERRY is 10 years old and lives in Chicago. Brielle likes to draw and paint and is really good at ballet. She wants a Barbie Dream House so she can have two and play sleepover. If she could have any superpowers, it would be mind reading and flying. Mind reading because if a villain thinks, "I'm going to shoot lasers at you," Brielle will know.

ERIC ARTURO BUSTAMANTE is 10 years old and lives in Chicago. Eric likes to play soccer and is really good at playing ultimate frisbee. He wishes to become a famous soccer player. If he could have any superpower, it would be to fly. When Eric grows up, he wants to be a famous dancer.

BLANCA RAQUEL CHIMBO is 11 years old and lives in Chicago. She likes to read *Diary of a Wimpy Kid* books eight, nine, and ten. She is really good at decorating and coloring. Blanca wishes for a lot of shoes and clothes. If she could have any superpower, it would be invisibility. When Blanca grows up, she wants to have two cars.

ALEXIS GERALDO CORRAL is 10 years old and lives in Chicago. Alexis likes to play Xbox One games and is really good at soccer. He wishes to be a millionaire with a pet phoenix. If he could have any superpower, it would be superspeed. When Alexis grows up, he wants to be a YouTuber.

ALEXA CRUZ is nine years old and lives in Chicago. Alexa likes to sleep and is really good at playing on the swings. She wishes for a bike. If she could have any superpower, it would be to fly. When Alexa grows up, she wants to work in a hotel.

BETHSAIDA CRUZ is 10 years old and lives in Chicago. Bethsaida likes to sing "Let it Go" a lot in her room. She is really good at soccer and basketball. Bethsaida wishes for a hoverboard because she rented one and liked it. If she could have any superpower, it would be to fly to see how it feels. When Bethsaida grows up, she wants to be a doctor because she wants to help people.

MELODY DORANTES is nine years old and lives in Chicago. Melody likes to play basketball and is really good at swimming. She wishes to invent time travel. If she could have any superpower, it would be to change her superpower whenever she wants. When Melody grows up, she wants to be an engineer and inventor. Melody also likes shopping for clothes and toys with her mom. She likes taking toys apart and putting them back together to see how they work with her dad.

EMILY DRZEWIECKI is 10 years old and lives in Chicago. Emily likes to play the zombie games on the Xbox and is really good at helping dogs get good homes at Hug-a-Pup every Saturday and Sunday. She wishes to have *Night Wolf*. If she could have any superpower, it would be to turn into any animal. When Emily grows up, she wants to be a pet shop owner.

RUBY NAOMI ECHEANDIA is 10 years old and lives in Chicago. Ruby likes to walk around her neighborhood and greet her neighbors. She is really good at doing people's makeup and is especially good at doing eyeliner. Ruby wishes she was a movie star in a dramatic film. If she could have any superpower, it would be the ability to freeze time. When Ruby grows up, she wants to live in a mansion that she would share with her family. Ruby loves pumpkin spice lattes from Starbucks.

MAURICE EDWARDS is 10 years old and lives in Chicago. Maurice likes to play video games and is really good at being funny and drawing. He wishes for an iPhone and a bowl of strawberry-vanilla ice cream. If he could have any superpower, it would be to be as fast as lightning to go anywhere. When Maurice grows up, he wants to be a YouTuber to make it rain.

STEPHANY ELIZALDE is 10 years old and lives in Chicago. Stephany likes to play outside with her friends and is really good at multiplying decimals. She wishes to travel around the world. When Stephany grows up, she wants to be a veterinarian.

ETHAN ESTES is 10 years old and lives in the Logan Square neighborhood of Chicago. Ethan likes to play hockey and is really good at *Team Fortress*. He wishes to be a defense-man for the Detroit Red Wings. If Ethan could have any superpower, it would be the ability to run on water so he wouldn't have to fly. When Ethan grows up, he wants to be a bio engineer. His favorite food is pizza.

SPARKLES FELICIANO is 10 years old and lives in Chicago. Sparkles likes to party and is really good at making toys. She wishes that any family will never be apart. If she could have any superpower, it would be all the superpowers in the world. When Sparkles grows up, she wants to be a firewoman.

ESTEBAN HEDIBERTO FLORES is 10 years old and lives in Chicago. Esteban likes to make funny comics and is really good at video games like *Minecraft*. He wishes to be very rich to buy a restaurant. If he could have any superpower, it would be to have a mechanical supersuit. When Esteban grows up, he wants to be a chef. His favorite food is pizza and his favorite drink is apple juice. His favorite school subject is technology.

SILVA JEAN FLORES is 10 years old and lives in Chicago. Silva likes to read any type of book, but especially books about Ancient Egypt. Silva is really good at simulation games, especially *Farm Story* from *Storm 8*. She wishes she had a lot of money. If she could have any superpower, it would be shape-shifting into anything. When Silva grows up, she wants to be an artist or writer.

ISABELLE CHRISTINA GARCIA is nine years old and lives in Chicago. Isabelle likes to play hide-and-seek and is really good at ballet. She wishes to have a rainbow pony. If she could have any superpower, it would be time traveling everywhere. When Isabelle grows up, she wants to be a math teacher in grammar school.

MARIE FLOWERS is 10 years old and lives in Chicago. Marie likes to play with her Barbies and is really good at playing with her American Girl doll. She wishes she had all the Shopkins. If she could have any superpower, it would be to fly and appear anywhere. When Marie grows up, she wants to be famous for the being best actress.

KIANA GRAYER is 10 years old and lives in the suburbs. Kiana likes to get money and buy toys and is really good at singing and acting. She wishes to become Taylor Swift's friend and become famous for her singing. If she could have any superpower, it would be to time travel and her BFF Brielle would have it, too. When Kiana grows up, she wants to become a chef or a nurse. If she becomes a nurse, she would work with her mom.

CHRISTOPHER JORDAN GUEDES is 11 years old and lives in Chicago. Chris likes to play basketball with his family and is really good at video games. He wishes to have a sports car when he's older. If he could have any superpower, it would be telekinesis. When Chris grows up, he wants unlimited money because he has won a rare lottery.

NATALIE GUZMAN is 11 years old and lives in Chicago. Natalie likes to dance to hip-hop, bachata, merengue, cha-cha, cumbia, and many more, and she is really good at choreographing dances. She wishes to become a famous dancer and for her family to be happy about her accomplishments. If she could have any superpower, it would be to have witch powers. When Natalie grows up, she wants to have a happy life with a career of being a dancer and an actress.

LILLIANA MARIA HARRIS (L.M. HARRIS) is 11 years old and lives in Chicago. Lilliana likes to dance to her favorite band XO-IQ and is really good at writing fictional stories. She wishes to be president of the world! If she could have any superpower, it would be ice powers, flying, shooting fireballs out of her hands, and laser fingers. When Lilliana grows up, she wants to be President of the World or The Best Movie Director for Awesome Fantasy ADVENTURES!

SKY ANGELINA JIMENEZ is 10 years old and lives in Chicago. Sky likes to play teacher and is really good at taking care of dogs. She wishes to have a mansion in Sydney, Australia. If she could have any superpower, it would be to fly. When Sky grows up, she wants to be a third grade teacher. Sky's other hobby is painting fingernails. Sky wishes to be a mermaid.

MARVIN LAZO is 11 years old and lives in Chicago. Marvin likes to play video games and is really good at soccer. He wishes for money and if he could have any superpower, it would be teleportation. When Marvin grows up, he wants to be a lawyer or a YouTuber.

VIKTOR N. MLADENOV is 11 years old and lives in Chicago. Viktor likes to play video games that are strategic and have action and he is really good at math. He wishes to finish school, high school, and college. If he could have any superpower, it would be to teleport. When Viktor grows up, he wants to have a big house, handsome clothes, and a big safe with money.

EMILY MONRREAL is 10 $\frac{1}{2}$ years old and lives in Chicago. Emily likes to read big, long books like *Wonderstruck* and *Harry Potter* and is really good at doing decimal division. She wishes she could be better at decimal subtraction. If she could have any superpower, it would be to harvest plants so we could feed all the animals. When Emily grows up, she wants to be a veterinarian.

OSCAR MANUEL MONRREAL, JR. is 11 years old and lives in Chicago. Oscar likes to read comics and fantasy books and is really good at math, jump rope, and soccer. He wishes for everything to be a chocolate island, and for everything to be magic. If he could have any superpower, it would be speed, telekinesis, teleportation, superstrength, and hypnotization. When Oscar grows up, he wants to be a chemical scientist. Oscar has healing magic.

MARITZA MORENO is 11 years old and lives in Chicago. Maritza likes to play *Growtopia* and is really good at soccer. She wishes to meet Neymar Jr., the Brazilian soccer player. If she could have any superpower, it would be telekinesis. When Maritza grows up, she wants to be a veterinarian.

ALEX MOROCHO is 10 years old and lives in Chicago. Alex likes to play *Growtopia* and is really good at soccer. He wishes to have an Xbox One to play *Call of Duty*. If he could have any superpower, it would be strength, speed, mindreading, and telekinesis. When Alex grows up, he wants to be a game maker, and to be in the Army.

JAIYA S. OVID is 10 years old and lives in Stinky Onion (Chi-town). Jaiya likes to swim and is really good at writing sci-fi. She wishes she could find a place where child authors go to connect in a separate magical world. If she could have any superpower, it would be swimming and running at the speed of light, and being able to breathe underwater. When Jaiya grows up, she wants to travel the world to places like Norway, Japan, and Scotland for fun and learning.

JOSHUA M. PARSIO is 11 years old and lives in Chicago. Josh likes to computer code and is really good at swimming backstroke, breaststroke, and freestyle races. He wishes he could go to a computer coding school. If he could have any superpower, it would be super speed and the ability to control water with his hands. When Josh grows up, he wants to be a video game designer.

FERNANDO PEREZ is 10 years old and lives in Chicago. Fernando likes to play soccer and is really good at video games. He wishes that everything he wanted was free for him, and if he could have any superpower it would be superspeed. When Fernando grows up, he wants to be a video game designer.

VIOLETA PEREZ is 11 years old and lives in Chicago. Violeta likes to dance to hip-hop and is really good at singing the Taylor Swift song "Wildest Dreams." She wishes to have snow fall on her birthday. If she could have any superpower, it would be to fly in the sky. When Violeta grows up, she wants to be a fourth grade math teacher.

SOPHIA RAMOS is 10 years old and lives in Chicago. Sophia likes to dance to hip-hop and is really good at dancing the bachata. She wishes to have a mansion and if she could have any superpower, it would be invisible transport. When Sophia grows up, she wants to be a dance teacher.

WILFREDO A. RAZO is 10 years old and lives in Chicago. Wilfredo likes to play video games with his friend and is really good at playing soccer. He wishes that he could teleport. If he could have any superpower, it would be robotic powers and the ability to fly. When Wilfredo grows up, he wants to be a hero/author.

AMARIS DIANA REYES is 11 years old and lives in Chicago. Amaris likes to play volleyball and is really good at painting nails. She wishes to live forever. If she could have any superpower, it would be to be a mermaid. When Amaris grows up, she wants to be a dolphin specialist.

JOANA REYES is 11 years old and lives in Chicago. Joana likes to make any kind of art, like paintings, and is really good at singing hip-hop. She wishes to be a billionaire. If she could have any superpower, it would be to have all of the superpowers in the world, especially invisibility and speedy strength. When Joana grows up, she wants to be a fifth grade teacher.

ALEXANDER JR. RODRIGUEZ is 11 years old and lives in Chicago. Alexander likes to watch Bulls games on TV and is really good at playing with his friends on the computer on the weekend. He wishes to learn to draw pictures of food. If he could have any superpower, it would be to give life and luck when he wants. When Alexander grows up, he wants to learn how to be a cop.

ANDRES RODRIGUEZ is 11 years old and lives in Chicago. Andres likes to play soccer at recess with friends and is really good at playing *FIFA*. He wishes to be 21 to get a house that has a bedroom and a computer. If he could have any superpower, it would be immortality. When Andres grows up, he wants to get a YouTube channel that's funny, and to make some money from the videos so he could make it rain and make people happy.

ANGELIZ RODRIGUEZ is 11 years old and lives in Chicago. Angeliz likes to play *Just Dance* and is really good at playing basketball. She wishes to own a toy store and play with the toys. If she could have any superpower, it would be to be invisible so she could sneak up on people. When Angeliz grows up, she wants to be an actress, singer, or doctor.

FRIDA ROTHEIM is 10 years old and lives in Chicago, Illinois. Frida likes to sing and is really good at soccer. She wishes to build a treehouse. If she could have any superpower, it would be to shoot flames out of her hands. When Frida grows up, she wants to be a doctor or a teacher.

SUNNIVA PETTERSEN ROTHEIM is 11 years old and lives in Chicago. Sunniva likes to play soccer and basketball and is really good at singing. She wishes to be in a funny movie. If she could have any superpower, it would be to run fast and to fly. When Sunniva grows up, she wants to be famous for acting in funny movies and singing pop songs.

ALONDRA RUVALCABA is 10 years old and lives in Chicago. Alondra likes to play with animals and is really good at playing outside and inside. She wishes to win billions and billions of money. If she could have any superpower, it would be to live forever. When Alondra grows up, she wants to be a professional gold medal Olympian.

BEYRALI SANTIAGO is 11 years old and lives in Chicago. Beyrali likes to watch TV and is really good at making jokes with her family. She wishes to be a vampire. If she could have any superpower, it would be time-stopping and transportation. When Beyrali grows up, she wants to be a fashion designer. Beyrali can speak Spanish and English.

KAYLA ELENA SANTIAGO is 11 years old and lives in Chicago. Kayla likes to play basketball and is really good at tennis. She wishes to just be herself no matter what people think. If she could have any superpower, it would be reading people's minds. When Kayla grows up, she wants to be a designer of beautiful pillows and dresses.

ORLANDO SANTOS is 11 years old and lives in Chicago. Orlando likes to play soccer with his friends and is really good at football. He wishes to play video games at his house with his friends from school. If he could have any superpower, it would be fire resistance and to live forever. When Orlando grows up, he wants to be a professional soccer player.

MARY STEINHOFF is 11 $\frac{1}{2}$ years old and lives in Chicago. She likes to make comics and is really good at styling hair. She wishes to take care of pit bulls (they are not scary) and if she could have any superpower, it would be to freeze water and turn it into lava! When Mary grows up, she wants to work in a shelter with dogs.

MIA TOLAYO is 10 years old and lives in Chicago. Mia likes to help people plan celebrations like Christmas, birthdays, and more. She is really good at making homemade salsa. She wishes to drive a car at the age of 14. If she could have any superpower, it would be to make music whenever she wants. When Mia grows up, she wants to be a doctor.

AMANDA VASQUEZ is 11 years old and lives in Chicago. Amanda likes to swim and ride her bike and is really good at watching TV series in one or two days. She wishes to go to Disney World. If she could have any superpower, it would be to have water and ice come out of her hands. When Amanda grows up, she wants to be a veterinarian or a cook.

ETHAN ANDREW VEGA is 10 years old and lives in Chicago. Ethan likes to watch *Pokémon* and is really good at entertaining his sister. He wishes for the world to live in peace. If he could have any superpower, it would be immortality. When Ethan grows up, he wants to be a YouTuber. His favorite food is steak.

LEODAN VENEGAS is 10 years old and lives in Chicago. Leo likes to play with a frisbee and is really good at playing soccer with his cousins. He wishes he was a minion. If he could have any superpower, it would be teleportation. When Leo grows up, he wants to be an astronaut because his mom says he is always on the moon.

GIMARY VILLATORO is 11 years old and lives in Chicago. Gimary likes to watch *Miranda Sings* on YouTube and is really good at painting pictures of nature. She wishes to be a famous actress. If she could have any superpower, it would be immortality because she wants to see the future. When Gimary grows up, she wants to be an actress for TV shows or movies.

About the Artists

ANDY BERLIN is 27 years old and lives in Chicago. Andy likes to make movies and is really good at drawing. He wishes everybody could just get along and if he could have any super-power, it would be flying without wings or jet propulsion. When Andy grows up, he wants to share the stuff he makes with everybody in the world.

COLE BLOTCKY is 29 years old and lives in Chicago. Cole likes to eat corn-dogs and is really good at cooking corn-dog pizza. He wishes corn-dogs grew on trees and if he could have any superpower, it would be the ability to time travel, but only to the year 1997. When Cole grows up, he wants front row tickets to every WWE Wrestle Mania event.

JEFFREY BROWN is 400 years old and lives in the mythical city of Chicago. Jeffrey likes to study Neanderthals and is really good at soccer, but maybe not as good as he likes to think he is. He wishes he could visit the moon and if he could have any superpower, it would be shooting lightning out of his fingertips. When Jeffrey grows up, he wants to live in a castle (he may never grow up, though!).

ASHLEY ELANDER is 28 years old and lives in Chicago. Ashley likes to draw and is really good at making people smile. She wishes every day was Saturday and if she could have any superpower, it would be teleportation. When Ashley grows up, she wants to make a living by drawing.

SICK FISHER is 30 years old and lives in Chicago. He likes to paint and play music with his friends and is really good at making sandwiches. He wishes for happiness and if he could have any superpower, it would be the ability to fly. When he grows up, he wants to be a professional artist.

JAY FLECK is 38 years old and lives in Shorewood. Jay likes to go running outside and is really good at drawing. He wishes there were 25 hours in a day and if he could have any superpower, it would be to cure people of disease. When Jay grows up he wants to be exactly where he is right now.

RYAN TROY FORD is 27 years old and lives in Chicago. Ryan likes to ride motorcycles and is really good at drawing flowers. He wishes everyone in the world could go camping together and if he could have any superpower, it would be the ability to make snacks appear on command. When Ryan grows up, he wants to be a cool dad with a big beard.

LYDIA FU is 1,000 years old and lives in Chicago. Lydia likes to dance to video game music and is really good at making potstickers. She wishes she could read every book in the world and if she could have any superpower, it would be to fly. When Lydia grows up, she wants to be an artist.

CHRISTOPHER BRYCE GIVENS is 24 years old and lives in Chicago. Chris likes to listen to records and is really good at playing video games. He wishes that he was having a picnic right now and if he could have any superpower, it would be the ability to fly like Super Flat Top Man, the comic he drew when he was nine. When Chris grows up, he wants to be his own boss.

SANYA GLISIC is one blaazzzillion years old and lives in Chicago. Sanya likes to run outside and is also really good at making art sometimes. She wishes to continue adventuring to remote, distant places and exploring as many new things whenever possible, and if she could have any superpower, it would be teleportation. When Sanya grows up, she wants to be content and continually inspired by life and things around her.

STEVE HAMANN is 44 years old and lives in Evanston. Steve likes to draw and is really good at painting. He wishes he could have a new puppy and if he could have any superpower, it would be the ability to fly. When Steve grows up, he wants a robot puppy.

PHINEAS X. JONES is 43 years old and lives in Chicago. Phineas likes to draw and is really good at nothing much else. He wishes his cats could help pay the rent and if he could have any superpower, it would be invisibility. When Phineas grows up he wants mostly impossible things.

SAM KIRK is 34 years old and lives in Chicago and Brooklyn. Sam likes to draw and paint and is really good at building things with wood. She wishes to travel the world to meet all kinds of new friends and if she could have any superpower, it would be to have green thumbs so powerful they could grow plants anywhere, on a moment's notice. These plants would feed our homeless. When Sam grows up, she wants to marry the woman of her dreams and have a family filled with love.

TJ KISER is 28 years old and lives in Chicago. TJ likes to draw and is really good at making people laugh. He wishes that everyone could get along and if he could have any superpower, it would be to make anyone smile. When TJ grows up, he wants to be a racecar driver.

KEARA MCGRAW is 23 years old and lives in Chicago. Keara likes to run next to trees and is really good at baking scones (sometimes). She wishes she could raise an eyebrow and if she could have any superpower, it would be the ability to talk to animals. When Keara grows up, she wants to draw every day and cook delicious dinners for herself every night.

MEGAN M. PELTO is 22 years old and lives in Chicago. Megan likes to read and is really good at illustrating. She wishes she could adopt all the animals and if she could have any superpower, it would be the ability to teleport anywhere in the world. When Megan grows up, she wants to be an illustrator and designer with at least one pet.

THOMAS QUINN is 35 years old and lives in Winnetka. Thomas likes to go to hockey games and is really good at broom-ball (yes, it's a real thing). He dreams of eating at a McDonald's on every continent and if he could have any superpower, it would be to never have to sleep.

MORGAN RAMBERG is 25 years old and lives in Chicago. Morgan likes to make moving things on the computer and is really good at cooking vegetarian stir-fry while listening to history podcasts. She wishes she knew how to code, and if she could have any superpower, it would be to have public speaking skills. When Morgan grows up, she wants to be a responsible dog owner.

KYRSTIN RODRIGUEZ is 22 years old and lives in Chicago. Kyrstin likes to eat and is really good at cooking. She wishes food wasn't so expensive and if she could have any superpower, it would be to fly so she could travel around the world and eat different kinds of food. When Kyrstin grows up, she wants to publish books, including illustrated recipe books!

ISABELLA ROTMAN is 24 years old and lives in Chicago. Isabella likes to draw comic books and is really good at doing mermaid stuff like swimming and tempting sailors into big scary rocks. She wishes her roommate's cat would stop eating her plants and if she could have any superpower, it would be to shape-shift into any animal, because then she'd have the power to fly, be super small, or be super strong all in one. When Isabella grows up, she wants to grow a tail and live in the ocean with the other happy sea monsters.

RICH SPARKS is several years old and lives in Chicago. Rich likes to make things out of wood and is really good at gardening. He wishes he had more hair and if he could have any superpower, it would be the ability to do laundry with his mind. When Rich grows up, he wants to be half an inch taller.

LAURA SZUMOWSKI is 32 years old and lives in Chicago. Laura likes to go hiking and is really good at riding bikes and dancing. She wishes she could attend Hogwarts School of Witchcraft and Wizardry and if she could have any superpower, it would be changing the weather. When Laura grows up, she wants to illustrate more books.

KELSEY ZIGMUND is 31 years old and lives in Chicago. Kelsey likes to frequent the city's many pastry shops and dog parks and is really good at color-coordinating. She wishes her dog, Toby, could talk, and if she could have any superpower, it would be to communicate with animals. When Kelsey grows up, she wants to live in Europe and hang out by the sea and eat many croissants.

JEFF ZIMMERMANN is 45 years old and lives in Chicago. Jeff likes to ride his bike and is really good at Spanish. He wishes for an excuse to go to China and if he could have any superpower, it would be flying. When Jeff grows up, he wants to live on the beach in Mexico.

Acknowledgments

This project and this book would not have been possible if it were not for the extraordinary trust and partnership of the students, teachers, and administration at Brentano Math & Science Academy. A massive round of applause to classroom teacher Mark Harlan, principal Seth Lavin, as well as Brentano educators Rosa Arce, Norma Ortiz, Emily Thies, Margaret Lopez, and Miki Son. Special recognition goes to our student editorial board members: Lilliana Maria Harris, Joshua Parsio, Chris Guedes, Kayla Santiago, Alondra Ruvalcaba, Marvin Lazo, Silva Flores, Maurice Edwards, Vanessa Benavides, and Emily Drzewiecki. Enormous thanks and gratitude also extends to the families and caregivers of our student-authors.

We are incredibly grateful for the generosity of AT&T Aspire, who helped fund this project. Thank you for giving our students the opportunity to become published authors and to share their stories with the world. You have helped change their lives, while enriching the lives of our wider community of staff, families, school partners, and volunteers. A big thank you also goes out to 826 National for their ongoing support of 826CHI's publication projects.

We offer a raucous round of applause to the inimitable Alban Fischer, who designed this book's cover and layout, including the two little monster mascots who cheer for our students' words throughout. Our sincerest gratitude goes to Joe Meno, one of our favorite Chicago authors who wrote a fantastic foreword championing the power of the imagination. The ever-talented Jasmin Shah made several visits to Brentano to photograph these student-authors, and for her time and expertise we are deliriously thankful. A combination high-five/hug combo goes to the talented crew of artists and illustrators who contributed gorgeous original works to accompany students' stories: Andy Berlin, Cole Blotcky, Jeffrey Brown,

Ashley Elander, Sick Fisher, Jay Fleck, Ryan Troy Ford, Lydia Fu, Christopher Givens, Sanya Glisic, Steve Hamann, Phineas X. Jones, Sam Kirk, TJ Kiser, Keara McGraw, Megan Pelto, Thomas Quinn, Morgan Ramberg, Kyrstin Rodriguez, Isabella Rotman, Rich Sparks, Laura Szumowski, Kelsey Zigmund, and Jeff Zimmermann.

Our incredible staff, who juggle multiple universes in their hands at all times, found the space to help edit, encourage, tutor, and visit Brentano's classrooms. Thank you to our entire 826CHI team for climbing aboard the Monster train with us, and a special shoutout to Abi Humber, who visited with journalists Aimee Leavitt and Jamie Ferguson to interview student-authors throughout the writing process.

We offer extra-special thanks to yearlong Publications Intern Alex Borkowski, who played crucial and multiple roles throughout the entirety of this project. Alex, your creative energy, relentless enthusiasm, and wholehearted belief in the power of student voice have given *OMG!* a life and vitality of its own. We also offer sincere gratitude to veteran volunteer Bryce Parsons-Twesten, who diligently built relationships with Chicago artists and illustrators on our behalf and whose vision offered the creative spark for this book project. Thank you, Bryce, for encouraging young people to tell stories and get lost in their imaginations.

We are forever indebted to and grateful for everyone who volunteers or interns with 826CHI—with such a small staff, there is no way we could accomplish even half of what we do without you, and we wouldn't have nearly as much fun. Cheers to each and every intern and volunteer who made weekly visits to work directly with Brentano students in their classrooms and/or spent hours typing, copy editing, and proofreading. We're talking about Kim Keating, Willie Filkowski, Torrie Fox, Julia Collins, Katy Laguzza, Brian Samuels, Molly Sprayregen, Josephine Mathias-Porter, Rachel Berg, Matt Gillespie, Mary Beth Higgins, Kelly Arrington, Chris Rife, Rosanna Turner, Daniel Evola, Maggie Embick, Zak Breckenridge, Sean Little, Brad Bauman, Sarah Smith, Imaan Yousuf, Kortney Morrow, Julia Collins, Kinsley Koons, Sarah Kokernot, Tracy Woodley, Reed Redmond, Steph Jurusz, Jac Kuntz, Matt Carmichael, Martii Kuznicki, Erin Vogel, Eric Van Orman, Fareine Suarez,

Lindsey Anderson, and Phil Morehart. *Thank you* for working tirelessly to make everything we do so much better.

Finally, to our readers: thank you for taking the time to value the work of these students. These stories are windows into our collective imagination, and they speak to our deepest fears and wildest dreams. If we can ask one favor, please do not simply read this book and place it carefully back onto your well-organized bookshelf. Share it with a friend. Read it aloud to strangers on a bus. Give it as a gift to someone you love. Set these monsters free!

About 826CHI

826CHI is a nonprofit organization dedicated to supporting students ages six to 18 with their creative and expository writing skills, and to helping teachers inspire their students to write.

Our services are structured around the understanding that great leaps in learning can happen with one-on-one attention, and that strong writing skills are fundamental to future success.

With this in mind, we provide after-school tutoring, creative writing workshops, in-schools residencies, field trips, and produce student publications. All of our programs are challenging and enjoyable, and ultimately strengthen each student's power to express ideas effectively, creatively, confidently, and in their own voice. Learn more at: **WWW.826CHI.ORG**.

MANAGING EDITORIAL TEAM

Alex Borkowski

Abi Humber

Amanda Lichtenstein

Bryce Parsons-Twesten

STUDENT EDITORIAL BOARD

Vanessa Benavides

Emily Drzewiecki

Maurice Edwards

Silva Flores
Chris Guedes
Lilliana Harris
Marvin Lazo
Joshua Parsio
Kayla Santiago
Alondra Ruvalcaba

About the Wicker Park Secret Agent Supply Co.

826CHI shares its space with the Wicker Park Secret Agent Supply Co., a store with a not-so-secret mission. Our unique products encourage creative writing, imaginative play, and trigger new adventures for agents of all ages. Every purchase supports 826CHI's free programming, so visit us at 1276 N. Milwaukee Ave in Wicker Park or online at **www. SECRETAGENTSUPPLY.COM** to pick up spy glasses, fake moustaches, our latest student-authored publications, and much more!

Monster-O-matic

A STEP-BY-STEP GUIDE TO WRITING YOUR VERY OWN MONSTER STORY

by MARK HARLAN & AMANDA LICHTENSTEIN

Brainstorm-O-matic

What are monsters? What do monsters teach us about humanity? How can we translate our fears into potential monster stories?

Take a look at images of beasts, mythical creatures, and monsters. What do these images make you think about or feel? What do monsters and beasts teach us about being human? Read *Life Doesn't Frighten Me* by Maya Angelou. What does Angelou's poem teach us about our own personal fears?

Key Vocabulary / Goals:
Brainstorm. Imagine. Gather ideas. Gather inspiration. Ask big questions. Make a list. Research. Free write.

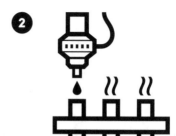

Character-O-matic

You've seen other monsters out there, and now it's time to invent your own.

Create a "Monster Bio" by answering the following questions: What does your monster look like? What are their habits, fears, secrets, and desires? What are three adjectives that describe your monster? Where does your monster live and how do they get around? What's your monster's worldview? What does your monster need more than anything in the world? What's getting in its way? What is an average day in its life?

Key Vocabulary / Goals:
Character. Sensory details. Description. Desire. Want. Point of view. Fear. Secret. Dream. Wish. Attitude. Personality.

3

Plot-O-matic

Now that you know your monster, it's time to outline a plan for your story and get started with a first draft. Let's imagine the possibilities. Where, when, and how does your story begin? What's the main conflict or problem in your story? What's the ultimate moment in your story? How do you imagine your story might end? Make sure you clarify your ***setting, characters (protagonists, antagonists), conflict, rising actions(s), climax, falling action(s) and resolution.***

Key Vocabulary / Goals:
Setting. Character. Protagonist. Antagonist. Problem. Conflict. Rising action. Climax. Falling action. Resolution.

4

Scene-O-matic

You have a basic outline for your monster story. You're ready to imagine what happens, scene by scene, ***action by action***. Think about ***the way*** something happened. Think about exactly ***how*** something happened. What do you see in your "mind's eye?" How would these scenes appear in the imaginary film of this moment? The more vivid and linked, the better. In each scene, make sure to include the three D's of great storytelling: ***Details, Description, and Dialogue.***

Key Vocabulary / Goals:
Details. Description. Dialogue. Actions.

Revise-O-matic

How's your story going? Now is the time to think about **structure, paragraph breaks, word choice, figurative language (similes, metaphors, onomatopoeia), logic, and sequence.** Read your story out loud to a trusted listener. Does it make sense? Do you need to add more details or description? Can you throw in a juicy comparison? Would dialogue help clarify a point of view? Make those crucial changes to let your story shine. Don't give up—you're almost done! This is the time to check for **spelling** and **grammar** mistakes. Not sure? Ask a trusted reader to help you **copy edit** and **proofread**. Don't forget your **title**—make it intriguing so readers will be enticed.

Key Vocabulary / Goals:

Structure. Paragraph breaks. Word choice. Figurative language. Similes. Metaphors. Onomatopoeia. Logic. Sequence. Copy edit. Proofread. Spelling. Grammar. Title.

Bio-O-matic

You've worked hard on your story and now it's time to give yourself well-deserved credit. Write an "Author Bio" in **third person** that includes important information like your name, age, where you live, what you're good at doing, and what you hope to be when you grow up. Your audience wants to know who you are, and it's time to celebrate!

Key Vocabulary / Goals:

Author. Biography. Third person.

7

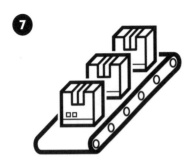

Share-O-matic

You've worked for hours to write a story that's vivid and descriptive. Congratulations on your final draft! Well done! Now, give your readers a monstrous gift by sharing your monster story with friends and family. Publish your work by making copies and passing them around. Hold a living room reading or backyard salon. Let your writing be heard by people who know and love you. You'll be a monster star!

Key Vocabulary / Goals:
Read. Share. Publish.

8

Reflect-O-matic

Phew! It's not always easy being a writer, but you made it. You wrote a story and shared it with others. How does it feel to write your own story? What would you do differently next time? What kinds of changes would you make to your story now? How could you tell this story from a different point of view or time period? What's your favorite kind of story to write? Don't wait too long . . . we can't wait to read your next story!

Key Vocabulary / Goals:
Reflect. Dream. Imagine. Gather new ideas. Gather new inspiration. Ask new big questions.